"Practical as well as beautiful."

"Stop."

"Stop what?" Without thinking, Ben pushed back the curl that fell into her face.

Heather willed her knees to return to their previous solid state and concentrated on the words and not the butterflies that were materializing.

"That," she said thickly. "You don't have to say nice things to me."

"Why wouldn't I want to say nice things to you?"

Words floated away from her brain like so many shards of ice, melting into nothingness. She shrugged. "You don't have to."

"Why don't you leave that decision to me?" he suggested.

Before she could answer, before she could even draw a single breath into her suddenly grossly oxygen-depleted lungs, Ben was framing her face with his hands, mingling her space with his own.

And then, just like that, there was no space left between them at all.

Dear Reader,

Well, by now you must have realized that I hate letting go. The last book in this series was supposed to be the last book. However, a reader wrote and asked me what happened to Shayne's brother, Ben, the man who in effect was the reason behind the series in the first place. I never had any intentions of giving him his own story—until I was faced with saying goodbye to Hades permanently. And then, I began to think that this might be a perfect way to end the series, to bring it full circle to Ben, whose flight from Hades was the reason for his brother eventually finding the love of his life. So here now is Ben, an older, wiser, contrite Ben, back after all this time to make amends because he, like that little girl with the scarlet shoes ahead of him, has come to realize that there's no place like home and nothing like family.

I wish you all much love in your lives,

Marie Ferrarella

MARIE FERRARELLA

THE PRODIGAL M.D. RETURNS

Silhouette®

SPECIAL EDITION®

Published by Silhouette Books

America's Publisher of Contemporary Romance

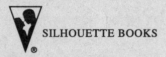

SILHOUETTE BOOKS
®

ISBN-13: 978-0-373-24775-2
ISBN-10:   0-373-24775-3

THE PRODIGAL M.D. RETURNS

Printed in U.S.A.

Books by Marie Ferrarella in Miniseries

MARIE FERRARELLA

This *USA TODAY* bestselling and RITA® Award-winning author has written over 150 books for Silhouette, some under the name Marie Nicole. Her romances are beloved by fans worldwide.

To Katherine Orr,
with thanks.

Chapter One

The warm, late-June breeze ruffled Ben Kerrigan's dark-blond hair as he raised his hand to knock on the door of the rustic, two-story house that stood just outside of the town of Hades, Alaska. This was the house where he had grown up. The house he had abruptly left early one morning seven years ago.

He'd been standing on the porch for the past few eternal moments, and he'd already raised his hand twice. His knuckles had made no contact with the weathered wood either time. Instead he'd dropped his hand to his side, as if all the energy had drained out of it.

Cowardice was something new for him.

For most of his thirty-four years, he'd sailed swiftly and happily through life. He'd had so much zest, it all but oozed out of him. Yes, there'd been mistakes, a whole host of them. God knew he would be the first to admit that, but somehow he managed to continue sailing because somehow, almost magically, difficulties always managed to get smoothed over.

A rueful smile twisted his lips as he stared at the door. In large part, the "smoothing over" had been due to Shayne, his older brother, the brother who had watched out for him, who'd raised him from the time their parents had died. Shayne had been the one who'd worked like a dog to put Ben through medical school so that when he graduated, he would return and work alongside him in the tiny medical clinic that was the only one of its kind within a hundred-mile radius. It was Shayne who had always been there to pick up the slack, the pieces, to fix whatever it was that needed fixing for him.

He hadn't seen Shayne for seven years now.

Hadn't seen Shayne or heard from him. Not since he had left town with Lila when she'd unexpectedly told him that she'd marry him, but only if they left Hades. That was seven years ago.

So he left with her. He'd run off, leaving Shayne to cope not just with the myriad of patients at the clinic, but with the two children that his ex-wife's recent death had deposited on his doorstep—two children he hadn't been allowed to see since almost infancy.

Then there was the woman that Ben had asked to come up to Hades. To marry him. That had evolved almost without his realizing it, at a time when his relationship with Lila had seemed impossible. The woman had written to him, commenting on an article he'd written in a travel magazine. He wrote back. One thing led to another and it turned into a love affair rooted in words. Photographs had been exchanged, but they had never laid eyes on each other before he'd proposed and she had accepted.

Looking back, he knew he'd been impetuous, but that was the way he'd always conducted himself. That word, more than any other, best described him. *Impetuous*. He'd tried to work on this in recent years. Especially this past one, after Lila walked out on him again.

The back of his neck prickled and he rubbed his hand over it, shifting uncomfortably, but remaining where he was. In front of the door. Knowing he had to knock, yet not being able to quite get himself to do it.

Having Lila walk out on him had taught him that being impetuous sometimes carried with it undesirable consequences. Waking up alone in their house had accomplished what years of Shayne's lectures hadn't. It had brought home the fact that he needed to become a little more responsible.

Hell, a lot more responsible. And he had, as time went on. Remaining in Seattle, he'd managed to attach himself to a very lucrative medical practice.

Working there with four other partners soon gave him everything he'd ever wanted.

Everything except a feeling of satisfaction.

Satisfaction continued to elude him, and this bothered him no matter how much he told himself it didn't.

As each month passed, his feeling of emptiness became stronger.

And the women who passed through his life didn't seem to matter. Sadly, they became interchangeable, their faces never leaving an impression on his mind. On his soul. Something else gnawed away at him. Something that went beyond primal appetites. He realized that there had to be more to life than this.

Ben began to think of himself in terms of the main character in Coleridge's epic poem, "The Rime of the Ancient Mariner." Though his outward demeanor never changed, inside was a different story. Inside he needed to atone for what he had done. He needed to find peace.

And then one evening, it came to him. He understood the source of his unrest. And, quite possibly, saw the source of his eventual healing.

On one of the public stations, there'd been a week devoted to Mother Nature's natural disasters. Leading off had been a story about cave-ins. One of them had lasted perhaps a whole ten seconds and had occurred in Hades, his hometown. It wasn't even a recent cave-in, just part of some old footage captured by a local station about mine cave-ins around the country and how they still occurred with more frequency than anyone was happy about.

That night, as he sat on the edge of his chair, recalling events from his childhood, he thought of Shayne. Shayne, who'd undoubtedly been in the thick of it, working madly to help with the wounded. Shayne, battling to make things right, the way he always did, and doing it almost single-handedly. Because that was the way Shayne was, a little larger than life and working for the good of others.

Ben had switched off the set and sat in the dark, thinking. Wrestling with his conscience. Shayne had always been there for him. It was time to be there for Shayne.

On the trip from Seattle to Hades, the last leg of which had been on a private plane he'd managed to hire for the drop-off, Ben had gone over this scenario more than a hundred times in his mind. He would appear on Shayne's doorstep, knock and then be enveloped in a reunion. He figured there'd be an initial awkwardness, quickly followed by his own heartfelt apology and Shayne's swift forgiveness. Shayne had forgiven him before.

He'd been confident that things would go back to the way they had once been.

But now that he was standing here, with the sun still casting shadows on the ground despite its being close to nine o'clock at night, he wasn't so confident anymore. The cheerful, devil-may-care attitude that had been the hallmark of his entire life had almost entirely deserted him. In truth, his confidence had been in rather short supply this past year, although he'd done his best to hide it.

Ben stared at the door. Damn it, he should have remained in contact with Shayne over the years. He should have sent a card that first Christmas, a card with a lengthy apology for having left his brother with such a mess to deal with. He'd been almost narcissistic then. He wasn't now.

Yet hindsight didn't change the past.

And each year that he hadn't sent that card or made that apology had made it that much harder for him to reestablish contact. Under normal circumstances he might not be making this attempt now.

But that cave-in program had brought things home to him in large, glaring letters and, what was more important, he now had a sense of his own mortality. A month ago he'd almost become a statistic. Another statistic in a lengthy list of traffic fatalities. He had been in the same kind of accident that had claimed the lives of his parents all those years ago. He felt as if someone or something was putting him on notice. He had allowed too much time to go by and wanted to spend the rest of his days with the only family he had: his brother, Shayne.

He needed to set things right. If that meant crawling, so be it. He'd crawl. Shayne had earned it.

Taking a deep breath, Ben raised his hand, and

this time he knocked. Knocked hard. Before his courage fled again, before his arm returned to the consistency of overcooked spaghetti.

He heard a noise on the other side. Shayne, he thought. He hoped he hadn't woken him up. Shayne was prone to grabbing catnaps whenever he could. There were huge demands placed on the town's only doctor.

A fresh wave of guilt swept over Ben. I'll make it right, he vowed. Shayne wasn't going to have to shoulder this alone anymore.

As the door opened, Ben's mind suddenly went blank. He searched for the right words that would put the past behind them and allow them to move forward. And yet, he couldn't form an appropriate greeting. Especially when Ben found himself looking not at his brother but at a woman. A slender, petite woman with long blond hair, lively blue eyes and a heart-shaped face that seemed to exude warmth. The breathtaking sight nudged at something buried deep within his memory banks. But at the moment he couldn't capture the elusive fragments.

"You're not Shayne," he heard himself say rather dumbly.

Sydney Elliott Kerrigan stopped drying her hands and stared at the man standing rather uncertainly on her doorstep. Strangers were not a common occurrence in Hades. The town and its surrounding area were not exactly on the beaten path. Outsiders did not usually trickle in unless to visit a relative.

Yet, as she looked at him, some vague familiarity fluttered along the perimeter of her memory, softly whispering that this man was not a stranger. She knew him. But from where? When? Seattle? No connection sprang to mind. She replied, "No, I'm not Shayne," to his surprised statement. Her smile widened as she struggled to place his face in the pages of her memory. "Are you looking for the doctor?"

Ben made no answer and wondered if he had the right house. He took a step back to glance at the front of the house, even though he knew in his soul that he hadn't made a mistake, hadn't lost his way.

But if this was still Shayne's house, who was this? She wasn't anyone who'd been living in Hades when he'd left town.

Sydney drew in her breath as her memory clicked into place.

The tall man standing before her, now slightly older and more sober looking, had been in the photograph she'd held in her hand as she'd gotten off the plane seven years ago. She'd come to Hades looking for a new life. Looking for happiness. On the strength of his letters and his proposal, she'd quit her job, terminated the lease on her apartment and packed all her worldly goods into a moving van to send them off to Hades.

Her heart stopped for a moment as recognition took hold. This was the face of the man who'd wooed her to come out here and be his wife.

The face of the man who had not been here to meet her plane or her.

She needed one final verification. "Ben?"

How did she know him? Had Shayne mentioned him, shown her a picture? "Yes, I—"

And then Ben stopped, his eyes widening ever so slightly as, out of the blue, his mind made a connection.

"Sydney?"

But even as he asked, he knew who she was. Sydney Elliott. He'd seen exactly one photograph of her. She'd sent it to him in one of her long, eloquent handwritten letters. Curiosity outweighed his guilt. What was she still doing here after all this time? He had just assumed that Shayne would have met her plane the way he'd requested, explained the situation to her and then sent her back home with airfare and apologies.

Before he could speak further, Ben found himself enveloped in the woman's warm embrace. Stunned, his breath caught in his throat before he awkwardly put his arms around her.

Had she been waiting here all this time for him?

No, that wasn't possible. That went beyond the patience of Job and slipped straight into the realm of pure fantasy. There had to be some kind of explanation.

Maybe he'd made a mistake.

"Who is it, Sydney?" Shayne Kerrigan called out to his wife as he walked into the living room from the kitchen. Dog-tired after the hours he'd put in at the clinic, he sincerely hoped that this was a social call instead of someone needing his professional help.

Loosening her embrace, Sydney stepped back and looked at Shayne. "Have we got a fatted calf we could put on the spit?"

He dearly loved his wife, but he wasn't in the best of moods right now. Frowning, he came forward, crossing to the door. "What are you talking about, woman? What—"

Shayne stopped dead, staring at the man who was standing beside his wife. He felt as if he'd just seen a ghost.

And was still seeing him.

"Hello, Shayne." Ben flashed a broad smile at his brother. His insides felt like Jell-O. He supposed it was a sign that he'd grown up. He was no longer ignoring the consequences of his actions. And he certainly didn't feel himself to be the center of the universe. Though he wanted to shake his brother's hand, he found himself unable to move.

Shayne squared his shoulders, his face darkening. "What are you doing here?"

"Standing in our doorway," Sydney replied cheerfully. She obviously wanted to be the peacemaker. Hooking her arms through Ben's, she drew him across the threshold and into the house. "Come in, Ben." Releasing him, she closed the door behind her brother-in-law, acting as if there was no history, no awkward past to overcome. "Have you eaten? We finished dinner a couple of hours ago, but there's plenty to—"

Shayne had not moved an inch since recognition had set in. "Get out," he ordered, his voice low, his lips barely moving.

Sydney's head jerked around in Shayne's direction. Bad blood or not, she seemed stunned to hear her husband's inhospitable words. Shayne had been a taciturn man when she'd first arrived, as warm as one of the intricately carved totem poles that could be found dotting the harsh terrain. But beneath the hard exterior, she had discovered the soul of a man who cared, who was there for his neighbors and his patients, giving more than he ever thought to get back.

Locked within himself at an early age, Shayne had never been able to express his feelings in any way verbally other than what amounted to a monosyllabic growl. His caring came out in the way he tended to the sick and the wounded. Sydney had been the one who had helped him out of his self-made prison, who had helped him bond with the two children who hardly even knew their father.

During the seven years that she had been married to him, Shayne had slowly become more at ease with himself. While no one could have accused him of exactly being warm and toasty, his enormous capacity for compassion was no longer a matter of question but of record.

She frowned at him now. "He's your brother, Shayne."

Shayne looked at his wife in surprise. "He's the man who ran out on you, Sydney—on both of us—with nothing more than a note." His anger growing, he glanced at his younger brother. "One lousy note and nothing more. Not in seven whole years," he emphasized, moving closer to Ben. Cutting Sydney out of his line of vision. "What's the matter, Ben? Are you in trouble? Do you need money? Is someone after you? Some woman you promised the moon to and who isn't satisfied with being left behind like some discarded tissue?"

He had that coming to him, Ben thought. That and a great deal more. And if Shayne gave him a chance, he'd say so. He'd apologize in every way he knew how. Life was too short to leave things the way they were.

"No, I just wanted to see you. To tell you I was sorry."

Shayne gave no indication that the words made any impression on him. His brother continued to glare at him. "And then what?"

Ben felt as if he was standing at the very edge of a cliff, overlooking choppy waters. Any moment he could lose his footing and fall off. But he hadn't come here to play it safe. He'd come here to make amends.

"That's up to you."

Shayne snorted, shaking his head. Unconvinced.

He knew Ben could turn on the charm and let it flow like others turned on a faucet. He'd seen his brother do it over and over again, avoiding penalties for his actions from the time he was old enough to widen his soulful eyes.

"Very tender, Ben, but you'll forgive me if I don't believe you."

"Shayne." Sydney tugged on his arm.

"Damn it, Sydney, this is the man who jilted you. Who treated you as if you were just so much disposable dirt."

"This is the man who's responsible for the greatest happiness I've ever known," she informed Shayne firmly. "If it hadn't been for Ben, I would never have come up here. I would never have been in a position where I couldn't just pick up and go back to what had been my home. If not for Ben, I would never have met our two beautiful children, never been blessed with having them in my life."

Her eyes held his. "If not for Ben, I would never have met you." Her voice softening, she laced her fingers through his, her eyes never leaving his face. "I would never have given birth to our daughter or been as sublimely happy as I am right at this very moment."

The news hit Ben like a ton of bricks. The town's men outnumbered the women seven to one. Given Shayne's personality, he'd never thought his brother would get married. Ben's jaw dropped as he looked from the petite woman to his brother. "You married my brother?"

"Seemed like the thing to do at the time," Sydney said with a laugh that warmed the room. "Shayne was very lost."

Originally, she'd intended to remain until her furniture arrived. She was going to tell the movers to turn around and take everything back to Seattle. But by the time her furniture came, she had lost her heart to the stern doctor and his two motherless children. There was no way she would ever have gone back.

"And he definitely needed a woman's touch, because he wasn't doing all that hot on his own," she added with a twinkle in her eyes.

"I would have been fine," Shayne informed her, softening despite himself. "In time."

She slid her arms through her husband's and leaned into him. "There's not that much time available in the whole world," she teased. And then, feigning a look of innocence, she asked, "Can he stay, Shayne? Please?"

The anger was already fading. When it came to Sydney, Shayne found he had trouble saying no. Even when he felt he should.

And when he allowed himself to admit it in the secret places of his soul, he had missed his brother a great deal. Worried about him and wondered what he was doing and where he had gone. It was like a wound that had refused to heal. Not knowing, not having any answers, had kept it that way.

"Yeah," Shayne mumbled grudgingly, his eyes still only on Sydney. "He can stay."

Chapter Two

"What are you really doing here?" Shayne asked as he closed the door to his den. Shayne had brought Ben into the small room, sealing them away from the rest of his family. He looked at him now, waiting for an answer.

Taking a seat on the creased dark-brown leather sofa, Ben looked around. And remembered.

The somewhat cluttered rectangular room, smelling of lemon polish and wood, hardly looked any different from when they'd played "fort" years ago, huddling beneath the scarred oak desk, pretending they were manning a fortress against some mysterious enemy. Back then the room with its stone fireplace had been their father's den and had smelled of cherrywood, the pipe tobacco their father favored.

Ben glanced at the wall adjacent to the fireplace. The floor-to-ceiling bookcase was jammed with books. His parents' library had been augmented with the medical books they both had pored over in school. His eyes came to rest on one shelf near the bottom. Instead of technical manuals or the classic literature that had belonged to their parents, the shelf housed what appeared to be a host of well-handled children's books.

His brother's life had a good balance to it, Ben thought. Unlike his own.

In his opinion, the last hour or so had gone rather well. Better than he'd anticipated when he'd first walked in. The children, Shayne's son and daughter from his previous marriage and the five-year-old product of his present union with Sydney had all taken to him.

Granted, the two older kids had been a little wary at first, and he could see they had their father's cautious approach when it came to people and trust. But the little one was different. She had climbed up onto his lap almost immediately, winning him over faster than he could win her. By the time he'd finished eating the meal Sydney had insisted on placing before him, Ben felt pretty certain he had been welcomed back into the family fold.

By everyone except the man he'd wounded most.

Crossing one ankle over a thigh, Ben selected his

words with care. He'd made peace with the fact that a great deal of effort was needed before Shayne would believe his sincerity. Before Shayne would stop looking at him warily, as if waiting for him to bolt.

But that was okay, Ben thought. He was prepared to go the distance. If Shayne wanted him to jump through flaming hoops, he'd jump through flaming hoops. He owed Shayne that much. And more.

"I already told you," Ben replied amiably. "I came back to apologize. And to make amends," he added. He watched as Shayne paced about the small room, never taking his eyes off his older brother.

"Suppose, for the moment, that I were to believe you." No clue in Shayne's voice let him know which way he was leaning. Turning sharply on his heel, he pinned Ben with a look. "Just how would you go about doing that?"

Ben met his gaze head-on, never wavering. "By staying here. By doing what you originally planned and working beside you at the clinic."

The words struck a faraway chord, nudging at memories that had belonged to the idealistic man Shayne had once allowed himself to be before seeing how foolish that was. He'd since made his peace with reality, striking an acceptable middle path. And then had become incredibly surprised when Sydney had come into his life and he'd discovered that life actually had more to offer. But this wasn't about him; this was about Ben. And Ben was about irresponsibility.

Shayne's eyes narrowed as he glared at his younger brother. He wasn't going to be taken in so easily. "When was the last time you practiced medicine?"

An easy grin slipped over Ben's lips. "I don't have to practice, I've got it down pat." Seeing the exasperated look on Shayne's face, Ben immediately raised his hands in complete surrender to ward off any words or rebuke. "Sorry. I could never resist that line."

Shayne's face darkened. "Medicine's not a joke, Ben. Especially not here."

Ben's expression sobered. "No, it's not. You're absolutely right. And to answer your question, last week." He saw Shayne raise an eyebrow quizzically. "That's when I last practiced medicine. Last week. Wednesday."

Shayne waited for the punch line. When it didn't come, he provided it by recalling Ben's old tricks. "Playing doctor with a willing woman—"

"Has its rewards," Ben concluded freely. "But I wasn't playing, Shay," he insisted. "I was part of a medical group in Seattle. My specialty is pediatric care." He didn't add that it was a very lucrative practice. That by coming here he had walked away from an income that totaled almost half a million dollars a year. Shayne was not impressed by statistics like that. To Shayne it had always been about the healing, nothing else. "There were four of us in the partnership," he explained. "Andrew Bell specializes in orthopedics, Will Jeffries is an internist and Josiah Witwer is a cardiologist."

"And your specialty is children," Shayne repeated.

Ben couldn't tell if Shayne was interested or just going through the motions. He did know, though, that he'd missed Shayne. Missed him more than he'd ever realized. Missed, too, how good Shayne's nod of approval had made him feel. He needed that nod again.

"Yes," Ben answered, then added, "We'd all overlap, taking over if someone was away. But mostly we stuck to our fields of expertise."

Shayne nodded, his expression stoic. "Pay's good, I imagine."

There was no point to lying. "Pay's great. But this isn't about the pay, Shay," Ben insisted. "This is about coming back. About finding a place for myself."

No one knew better than Shayne how persuasive Ben could be. His charm had gotten him out of many sessions of detention, out of well-deserved punishments. He had a glib tongue and a Teflon body. There was no place for either in his clinic.

Reaching for the decanter of brandy he kept on his desk, Shayne poured a small glass for Ben and then one for himself. "We don't need someone who wants to put on a hair shirt for a week and then take off—"

"I'm not going to take off," Ben said, interrupting him. The smile on his lips had faded just a little. "I'm willing to do whatever it takes. I'm good, Shayne. You know that. I'll do whatever you need."

Shayne sat down on the edge of the desk and sipped his brandy slowly, watching his brother over the rim of his glass.

"What happened?" he finally asked.

Ben shrugged carelessly. "I grew up."

"I mean to Lila."

Ben took a breath, as if to brace himself against the words. Against the memory. "She left me," he said simply. Raising his glass in a silent toast, he took a healthy sip before lowering it again. "That was part of the growing process."

"Left you," Shayne said slowly, as if digesting the information. "Just like that?"

"Just like that." It still felt incredibly painful, more than a year later. It had taken him a year to get his act together, to take his feelings out of deep freeze. "One morning I rolled over in bed and reached out for her, but she was gone." There'd been just the shortest of notes to say that they were different people now and she was leaving because she was bored.

Shayne watched him for a long moment. He couldn't help feeling just the slightest bit vindicated. "Hard being disappointed in someone you thought you could count on, isn't it?"

He had that coming, Ben thought. But even so, he couldn't help the defensive response that rose to his lips. "I'm sorry that I hurt you, but you should have known better than to count on me back then. You were always the stable one."

Being the stable one was a quality that, though expected, was so easily taken for granted. At times, he felt like a roof, there to give shelter and never to be noticed. Not like Ben. "And you were the one everyone doted on."

"And the one nobody took seriously," Ben said. He took another long sip of brandy. The guilty feelings that had haunted him, that had brought him here, refused to be sublimated.

Shayne laughed shortly. "You didn't want to be taken seriously."

That was the boy he'd been. But he wasn't a boy any longer. "I do now." Putting down his glass, Ben looked his brother in the eye. "Whatever it takes, Shay. Whatever it takes," he repeated with feeling. "I want to stay in Hades."

Shayne gave no indication as to whether or not he welcomed his brother's presence. The suspicious glint in his eyes remained. "Someone suing you for malpractice?"

Ben shook his head. He had that coming, too, he supposed. That and a lot more. Time and again, he'd taken Shayne's trust and abused it. But he was here now and he was going to prove himself. No matter how long it took. "I'm a good surgeon, Shayne. A good doctor." His record was without blemish. Whatever else he might have been, he was always dedicated to his profession. "You could use the help."

"I have the help," Shayne countered. He poured himself a little more brandy, topping off Ben's glass. "Since you've been gone, I've taken on a nurse practitioner and she lured her brother to come settle here. He's a heart specialist. Jimmy Quintano."

Silence wove its way around the corners as Ben absorbed what his brother had just said. He'd never thought that anyone would actually come here. When he was growing up, everyone wanted to leave Hades. Everyone but Shayne and his friend Ike.

"Then the answer's no?" Ben finally asked.

"I didn't say that," Shayne said, warming the glass between his hands. "You can join me at the clinic. But we go by my rules."

Ben felt the way he had as a kid in the dead of winter when he finally saw a ray of sunshine slicing through the eternal darkness. He grinned at his brother. "Whatever you say."

"The first thing I 'say,'" he told Ben, finishing his drink, "is that the clinic opens at seven." He received the expected response from Ben, who looked properly sobered by the piece of information. "Something you'd like to say about that, Ben?"

Ben gave him a completely innocent look that didn't fool his brother for a moment. "Yeah, can I catch a ride with you?"

Shayne snorted. "Seeing as how you'll be

sleeping in the guest room tonight, I don't suppose that'll be a hardship."

Unable to contain his enthusiasm, Ben rose to his feet and embraced his brother. Shayne endured the contact, neither returning the embrace nor moving back to terminate it.

"It's good to be back, Shayne."

"We'll see, Ben. We'll see." The look on Shayne's face as they separated told Ben that his older brother was far from being won over yet.

But he would be, Ben promised himself silently.

He'd never been a morning person. Ever.

The two cups of extrastrong black coffee that were now infiltrating his veins, attempting to jolt his bloodstream into some semblance of attention, helped a little but not nearly enough. The swaying of the Jeep as Shayne drove them into town the next morning was all but lulling him back to sleep. It was a struggle to keep his eyes open.

When he realized that his lids had shut, he jerked his head up, but not before Shayne spared him a look. "I can still turn around and drop you off back at the house, Sleeping Beauty."

Ben shifted in his seat. "Nope, I'm fine."

Shayne laughed. "Yeah, for a zombie."

Busted, Ben yawned and stretched, rotating his shoulders. "Just takes me longer to come around, that's all." Shayne had always been just the opposite, getting up in what amounted to the middle of the night as far as he was concerned. Like the marines, his brother got more done before eight in the morning than most people accomplished all day. "Besides, I've always done my best work after twelve."

Shayne gave him a knowing look. "Yeah, I know."

For once he wasn't referring to anything that had to do with the fairer sex. He was being serious. "You know what I mean."

Shayne merely slanted a glance at him before pulling his Jeep into the first parking space located directly at the rear of the clinic.

They were here. He hadn't even realized it, Ben thought. Shayne had taken the shorter route, not through the town but the back roads, and they had approached the whitewashed, single-story building from the rear.

Getting out, Ben took in the building with its fresh coat of paint. The paint wasn't the only thing that seemed new. He followed Shayne up the back stairs as he unlocked the door. "Is it my imagination or—"

"We've added on," Shayne told him. "A couple more exam rooms," he specified, "and an O.R. for minor surgery. Anything major we still send them on to Anchorage General." That was one of the reasons he and Sydney had a single-engine plane, so that patients could be flown to the city if need be.

"More exam rooms," Ben echoed. "Is the town really growing?"

"Some," Shayne allowed. Walking in first, he waited for Ben to cross the threshold, then shut the door again. The clinic was almost eerily quiet. "We've had some new blood come in." Shayne went into his office. He took out his lab coat and put it on. As an afterthought, he reached in for his spare one and held it out to Ben. "And fewer people leave."

Ben slipped on the white coat. Almost like old times, he thought. "That new blood, is it responsible for the restaurant and emporium I saw when I was driving through?"

Shayne smiled to himself. By regular standards, the town was almost standing still. But as far as the citizens of Hades were considered, they were experiencing a building boom. An actual firehouse had been constructed less than a year ago, joining a renovated movie theater and a very small hotel.

"In part. Ike and Jean Luc have been investing in the town and adding buildings here and there."

"Ike? You mean the bartender at the Red Dog Saloon? Your friend, Ike LeBlanc?" Growing up, Ike and Shayne had been friends. He remembered the man as being outgoing and gregarious, while his cousin, Jean Luc, had been the quiet one. He couldn't picture either as entrepreneurs.

Shayne nodded, straightening the collar on his lab coat. "He's branching out."

Following Shayne into the main reception room, Ben shook his head. He never thought progress would come to Hades, a place that had seemed frozen in time when he'd lived here. "I've missed a lot, haven't I?"

"Yeah, you have. But you can catch up." Shayne realized that he shouldn't count on his brother so soon. Ben had a long way to go before he proved himself dependable. "If you're serious about staying."

"Very serious." Whatever else Ben was going to say was temporarily placed on hold as he looked out the window that faced the front of the clinic. He saw a willowy-looking blonde holding on to two little girls. The twosome seemed determined to pull as far away from each other as possible, taking their mother with them. He glanced at his watch again. A shade before seven. "Looks like you've got patients."

Shayne glanced at the appointment book that Alison had left opened for him on her desk. Right beside it was a computer tower holding the exact same information. Sydney teased him and called him her lovable dinosaur, but he'd always preferred paper and pen. It made him feel more hands-on and in control of a situation. Software could whimsically swallow up all the information just when he needed it most.

"That would be Heather and her two girls, Hannah and Hayley," Shayne told him.

"Heather?" The instant he repeated the name, bits and pieces of memories came flying back to him. Memories he realized he had all but forgotten. Memories that made him smile.

She looked thinner, he thought. And prettier, although definitely more harried.

"Heather Kendall. Ryan," Shayne clarified. He couldn't remember if Ben had left Hades before or after Heather had married Joe Kendall.

Ben stepped away from the window but continued to look at the woman and her daughters. All three were unaware that they were being observed.

"I know who she is."

Ben's quiet tone caught Shayne's attention. He vaguely recalled that there'd been something between Ben and Heather, but then, at one point or another there'd been something between Ben and every female under the age of fifty in Hades. Never mind that the men outnumbered the women in Hades by seven to one and any woman had her pick of men. Every female Shayne knew of had chosen Ben at one time, and he had chosen them.

About to unlock the front door, Shayne paused, looking at his brother. "You okay?"

Ben shook off the memory of one exquisite night by the lake and skin softer than silk.

"Like I said, I'm fine." He flashed a grin. "Nothing more coffee won't help."

"Coffeemaker's in the back," Shayne told him. "Feel free to pitch in. Alison hates making coffee." Flipping the lock, he opened the double doors and smiled down at the two energetic little girls. "Hello, Hannah, Hayley." He looked up at Heather. "You're early."

As she struggled with her daughters, who were now tugging harder, not just to avoid each other but to get away altogether, Heather offered Shayne a smile that was just a little weary around the edges.

"I know. Lily's giving me the morning off, but Beth just called me to say that she's not feeling well and won't be coming into the restaurant. That leaves Lily juggling the breakfast crowd on her own." Lily had been good to her, coming to her rescue when Joe was killed in the cave-in and offering her a job. She'd been the world's worst waitress, but Lily had stuck by her. Leaving her in the lurch was not the way to repay her. "I hate doing that to her."

Shayne shook his head. "If I know Lily, she'll get Max to wait on tables."

Max Yearling was Hades's lone law enforcement officer. He was also Lily's husband. Like Jimmy Quintano, Lily had come to Hades by way of Alison, who in turn had found her way to Hades because of Luc. Luc had gone to Seattle on vacation and on his first day there, had come to her rescue when someone had attempted to mug her. It was because of Luc she'd learned about Shayne and his clinic. Eager to make a difference, she'd come up to the tiny town to work. Her siblings had come to visit. And one by one, each had lost their hearts, not just to the land but to the people bound to it.

Shayne smiled to himself. In a way, the town's history was like one long, intricate nursery rhyme, with one family member following another. Hades now boasted of four Quintanos, three of whom were married to Yearlings, while Alison, who had come to him originally to become an accredited nurse practitioner, was now married to Jean Luc.

"I'd rather she didn't. I need the job," Heather told him, only half joking.

Hannah, her six-year-old, was struggling to break free and make a dash for the front parking lot. "I don't want a shot," Hayley protested vehemently, her lower lip quivering as tears began to fill her eyes.

"No shots today," Shayne promised. "Just a check-up to see if that nasty rash you and your sister have been passing to each other has finally cleared up."

"A nasty rash?" Ben repeated in mock disbelief as he came forward. He looked from one girl to the other, appropriately wide-eyed. "You two girls don't look as if you'd have a nasty rash."

"We did," Hayley, the more outgoing of the two, declared. She pointed a finger at her older sister. "Hannah got it first because she was playing in the bushes Mama told her not to."

Fear faded as Hannah took offense, embarrassed in front of the stranger. "Was not."

Hayley fisted her free hand at her waist the way she'd seen her mother do. "Was, too."

Ben got down on one knee, refereeing. "I bet that old bush just jumped up at you and grabbed you, didn't it, honey?"

The excuse clearly appealed to Hannah, who

nodded her blond head vigorously, sending her curls bouncing up and down. "Uh-huh."

"Gotta watch out for those magical bushes," Ben agreed. "They're fast. Where did it grab you?"

Hannah never hesitated. She pushed her sleeve up immediately, exposing her right arm. She pointed to an area that had been an angry pink only a couple of days ago. "Right here."

Still on his knee, Ben examined the area carefully. "Looks like it's gone to me."

"Mama rubs this yucky stuff on us," Hayley told him, moving aside her own sleeve to show him that her skin was clear as well.

"That's because she loves you." Ben looked up at Heather. "Right, Mama?"

Heather forced herself to nod her head, her eyes almost glued to the man talking to her daughters. Her voice had deserted her around the same time that the temperature in the room had gone up twenty degrees and the lights had suddenly dimmed to the point where she had to struggle to keep from slipping into darkness herself.

She could feel her heart pounding in her chest, its cadence echoing the refrain that kept repeating itself in her head: *He's back.*

Ben's back.

Chapter Three

"Looks like both your girls are doing very well," Shayne told Heather. Or the woman that had been Heather until a couple of minutes ago, Shayne thought as he glanced at the shell-shocked expression on her pretty face. Apparently he wasn't the only one who'd been caught off guard by his brother's sudden reappearance in town. "Heather," he added for good measure.

When the girls' mother gave no indication that she had even heard him, he repeated her name, a bit more forcefully this time. From all appearances, Ben had lost none of his magnetic pull nor any of his effect on women.

Shayne shifted until he was directly in front of her. Almost amused, he passed a hand in front of her face. It was a beat before she even blinked.

"Heather," he deadpanned, "how long have you had this hearing loss?"

It took all she had to pull herself out of the mental abyss into which she'd unexpectedly sunk. Shaking off the mental cobweb as best as she could, Heather looked at Shayne.

"What? Oh, I'm sorry, Doc Shayne, it's just that, well—" Words deserted her.

"Yes," Shayne said, glancing toward Ben, "he has that effect on all of us." There was only the slightest hint of sarcasm in his tone.

"No, no, I mean—" Flustered, Heather struggled to get a hold of herself. "I'm just surprised to see— to see Ben back, that's all." Trying to address Shayne, her eyes were still drawn to Ben as she spoke.

Damn, she was doing it again, tripping over her own tongue. But then, as her mother had enjoyed pointing out, she'd never been one of those women for whom composure was second nature. Composure wasn't even remotely residing in her neighborhood at the moment.

Heather made another attempt to collect herself. She wasn't that wide-eyed twenty-three-year-old Ben had made love with by the lake that last summer before he abruptly disappeared. She was years older than the seven that had passed. Life's requirements had done that to her. They had made her a mother twice over, as well as a wife, then a widow.

These days she found herself being a caretaker, her mother's keeper, in addition to being the sole support of her little family. Most of the time, she was also her mother's chief source of money, as well.

Her mother.

Oh, wow. Martha Ryan was going to have a lot of choice things to say once word of Ben's return reached her. Even if she said nothing to her mother herself, and she didn't really intend to, the woman would find out. Word always spread in Hades.

Anticipation coursed through her veins. Her mother had never liked Ben. Whenever she did mention his name, Martha Ryan always compared him to the husband who had first deserted her and then divorced her through a lawyer he'd retained in Wichita, Kansas. As she grew older, Heather ceased to hold her father's disappearance against him. Instead she began to understand why he'd gone. It had a great deal to do with self-preservation.

She felt Ben's deep-green eyes on her and did her best not to squirm. Not to react at all. She succeeded marginally. But then, she'd heard that stone statues reacted to his gaze.

Heather cleared her throat. "Are you back?" she managed to ask, fervently praying she'd sounded at least a little aloof.

Her cool demeanor, if attained, was spoiled by

Hayley's very plaintive and accusing wail. "Mama, you're squeezing my fingers off."

Heather instantly loosened her grip. "Sorry, baby," she murmured under her breath. Even as she uttered the words, she could feel several shades of pink dash up the sides of her throat. The colors spread even more rapidly to her cheeks.

"No need to hold on to her so tightly," Ben told her genially. He looked down at the younger girl. "She's not going anywhere, are you, Hayley?"

Hayley, like every female over the age of twelve months, instantly responded to both his tone and his smile. She shook her head madly from side to side, her eyes never breaking contact with his.

"Uh-uh."

The next moment she was tugging her hand away from her mother's grasp. The second she was free, she slipped her hand into his, accompanying the action with a huge smile aimed directly at him. Unknown to her five minutes ago, the man had suddenly become the center of her universe.

That's the way it usually was, Heather thought ruefully. Every girl she'd gone to school with had a crush on Ben.

He didn't remember her being this pretty, Ben thought. Or this silent. For a moment he forgot that Shayne was her doctor. "Do you have time for a thorough exam?" he asked her. When he saw Heather's eyes widen in surprise, Ben realized that he had left off a few crucial words that might make the difference. "Of the girls," he added. "Just to put your mind at rest."

Beside him, he heard Shayne's impatient intake of breath. He'd stepped on toes again. But no one else was in the clinic and there was time to be thorough. What he recalled most about practicing here with Shayne was that they'd always been rushed to see as many patients as they could within the space of a day.

"That's okay. You don't need to bother. The rash was only on their arms." It took everything she had not to turn and run, clutching her daughters to her. Her own voice sounded almost breathless to her as she answered.

C'mon, Heather, get a grip.

Heather tamped down an onslaught of erupting nerves. She needed to calm down before she made a complete idiot of herself.

Very carefully Ben examined the arms of first Hannah, then Hayley before making his pronouncement. He addressed his conclusions not to Heather, but to her daughters, who appeared to absorb his words as if they were tiny little sponges. Their eyes shone at being treated like adults.

"I'm happy to tell you girls that there's no rash here now. Guess the yucky medicine made it go away."

"Guess so," Hayley agreed, solemnly nodding her head.

Hannah said nothing, only looked at him with her

wide green eyes. When he returned her gaze, she suddenly turned shy, shifting closer to her mother. Though part of her face was buried in Heather's shirt, Hannah kept one watchful eye on him.

Heather pasted a smile on her lips as she turned to Shayne. "I guess this means I'm not going to be late after all." She glanced at her watch. "If I hurry to get the girls back home."

"Need a ride?" Ben offered. He was aware of the sharp look that his brother gave him. But it was too late to gracefully rescind his offer.

Heather was already edging her way over toward the front door, drawing Hannah with her. Hayley was another story. "I have my car."

"I'll go with him," Hayley volunteered eagerly, her eyes all but lighting up.

Shayne interceded. Without looking at Ben, he squatted down to Hayley's level. "Sorry, honey, but I need him here. He's a doctor," Shayne told her.

Hayley's perfectly shaped, tiny golden eyebrows knitted themselves over her nose as she pondered what Shayne had just told her. Looking up at her new hero, she asked, "You're like him?"

Shayne placed his hand on his brother's shoulder as if for the little girl's benefit. "He's working his way up," he responded before Ben could say anything.

Ben flashed a grin at his brother. "And I've got a long way to go."

"But you're bigger," Hayley pointed out in earnest, looking from one man to the other.

Amused, Ben assured her, "Size doesn't matter in this case." Glancing toward Heather, he noticed that Hannah was now burying her face in the fold of what there was of her mother's skirt.

Heather had a great pair of legs. But then, she always did have. He remembered watching her practice cheerleading moves on the field while he and his friends were supposedly listening to the coach give orders. He allowed himself a moment to appreciate the view. For old-time's sake.

"Is there anything else while you're here?" Shayne asked her.

Heather shook her head, a little emphatically in Shayne's estimation. "No. Thank you." She felt behind her for the doorknob. Finding it, she held on as if it represented her ticket to freedom. "I can pay you around the middle—"

Shayne waved away her words. "Follow-up care. See you girls later."

"Um, yes. Thank you," Heather stammered. With a quick nod at Ben, she turned on her heel and left the premises. She had to almost drag Hayley in her wake. The latter, her gaze intent on Ben, waved madly as she disappeared down the front steps of the porch.

Shayne waved back even though he knew that the attention was centered exclusively on Ben. The door closed and he turned to face his brother.

"Looks like you're a hit with the under-three-foot set," he commented. Glancing at the day's appointments, he saw that the next one wasn't scheduled for another half hour—provided there were no emergency phone calls.

He knew better than to count on that. But he did need a caffeine hit.

Since Ben had neglected to take his blatant hint about making coffee, Shayne made his way to the back room and the barren coffeepot. Of late, at a very minimum, he found himself averaging a cup an hour. It was an unabashed intent on his part to stave off exhaustion. The feeling seemed to haunt him more and more these days, though he kept that to himself. Given Sydney's penchant for reading him like a book, he knew it was only a matter of time before his "secret" was out. Hopefully, by then his energy would make a reappearance of its own volition.

"Not entirely," Ben replied, following him into the back. He leaned against the doorjamb, watching Shayne move about the cramped area. With a discarded dinette table in the middle, surrounded with four chairs, the room wasn't big enough for both of them to move around, and he didn't want to crowd Shayne. "Her older girl looks as if she's afraid of me."

"Hannah," Shayne said. "Hannah's shy. She's always been the quiet one in her family. She was born without making a sound." He smiled. "Heather used to bring her in, concerned because Hannah didn't cry. I told her to be grateful. Once Hayley was born, she realized she'd had a good thing with her firstborn."

Ben nodded, only half listening. Another question had occurred to him. Try as he might, he couldn't see the petite, delicate Heather married to Kendall, a big, burly man who looked far more at home handling steel beams than holding something as fragile as Heather in his arms. "How's Joe Kendall doing? Is he still a miner?"

"Not these days," Shayne told him dryly. Putting the filter in its proper place, he measured out several heaping tablespoons of coffee and then added very little water. The pot began making noises as it heated the water. "He's dead."

"What do you mean, 'dead'?"

"The usual definition," Shayne responded mildly. He replaced the plastic lid on the can of coffee and put it back into the tiny refrigerator Sydney had given him. "Not breathing. Body decomposing, or in Joe's case, already decomposed." He turned from the coffeemaker and glanced at his brother. "Did you sleep through the basic course in medical school?"

"I mean dead how?" Ben pressed. "How did her husband die?"

"Cave-in at the mines."

The words were recited without feeling, but Ben knew better. No one cared more than Shayne about these people. Whenever there was a cave-in, Shayne was the first there to help with the wounded. To go into the bowels of the earth if need be. Shayne coped by keeping a tight rein on his feelings. Just the way he had when their parents were killed.

Ben thought back to the special he'd watched last month. The one that had triggered his decision to return home. Maybe the footage he'd seen on the Alaskan cave-in had even been of the one that had claimed Heather's husband.

Small world.

He realized that Shayne was holding a cup out to him. Taking it, he looked down at the pitch-black, almost-solid contents. "You know, you should offer to coat the walls at the mines with this stuff, Shay. They'd never cave in again."

"Starbucks is approximately a hundred miles due east," Shayne told him, pointing in that general direction. Just as he took a sip of the dark brew, they heard a bell ring in the front. It was swiftly followed by a low, resonant greeting.

"'Morning!"

"That would be Jimmy." Rather than leave the cup behind, Shayne topped it off then headed out of the small room. "C'mon. Time to make introductions."

The coffee jolted through Ben's system. He'd forgotten just how strong Shayne's coffee could really be. He smiled to himself as he followed behind his brother. It felt good to be home.

Heather had no recollection of the short drive home from the clinic. She didn't remember getting into the car, didn't remember strapping the girls in, didn't remember starting the car or turning on the radio. As she paused to glance into the back, she was surprised to see the girls were each in their car seats where they were supposed to be. She vaguely became aware the radio was on only when she heard the deejay, Preston Foster, launch into his stale routine. It hadn't changed very much since he'd cut his teeth on the radio station in high school.

Staring ahead again, she gripped the steering wheel so tightly that had it been frozen, she would have succeeded in snapping it in two. Not to mention she was moving slightly faster than a snail suffering from a bout of the flu.

It was a preventative action because she didn't want to hit anything. The fact that Hades had no traffic seemed to have escaped her. At given times of the day, there would be only one, possibly two vehicles on any of the three streets that led in and out of the town. A traffic jam was declared whenever three vehicles all headed in the same direction.

"Faster, Mama, faster," Hayley urged. The girl waved her feet back and forth quickly, as if that would help propel the vehicle a little faster. "I'm gonna miss Celia Seal."

Trying not to think about the man in the clinic, Heather pressed down on the accelerator. The speedometer on the dash rose to a racing twenty-five miles an hour.

"We'll get there," Heather assured her younger daughter.

Hayley was unconvinced. "Shoulda let the doctor drive," she said, pouting.

Should have never come in today, Heather thought. "Maybe next time."

Glancing in the rearview mirror, she saw that Hayley's face had lit up as she strained against her restraints. Lack of enthusiasm had never been Hayley's problem. "Really?" she asked eagerly.

"No, not really," Heather told her quietly, struggling to tuck away the frayed ends of her nerves. "He has other things to do."

For now, Hayley dropped the subject and bounced on to another. "Do you like him, Mama?" she asked. "I like him. He's cute." She punctuated her declaration with a giggle, then tried to muffle the sound with both hands across her mouth.

Heather sighed, shaking her head. Like mother, like daughter. Except that she'd learned the hard way just what a fool she was. She fervently prayed that Hayley would never meet someone who would shake her world up so completely.

Looking again in the rearview mirror, she said to her older daughter. "How about you, Hannah?" Hannah had lapsed into her customary silence while they were still at the clinic. Heather had tried to gauge the little girl's reaction to Ben, but she couldn't detect anything one way or the other. "Do you like him?"

Hannah turned her small face toward the window at her side. Small shoulders rose and fell, as if she hadn't thought about it and now found the topic not crucial enough to consider.

Hayley's legs waved even faster. "Hannah doesn't like anybody," she declared.

"Do, too," Hannah protested.

And they were off, Heather thought. But at least they were home, she comforted herself. Turning the wheel, she pulled up right in front of the small two-story house that Joe had built for her with his own hands. It was a labor of love. Every time she looked at it, she could feel a smattering of guilt assail her. Joe had loved her a great deal. And she had rewarded that love with deception.

Not going to do you any good, dwelling on that. You did the best you could. For everyone.

Knowing that didn't make it right.

"Don't fight, girls," she said, turning off the engine. "You know how it bothers Gran."

"Everything bothers Gran," Hayley responded with a wisdom that was far beyond her four years.

She had that right, Heather thought. As far back as she could remember, her mother had something disparaging to say about almost everyone and everything. She tried to remember the last time she'd seen her mother smile, and couldn't. The woman's face had all but frozen in a permanently sour expression. It made her appear years older than the date on her birth certificate.

Heather stifled a sigh as she got out of the car and opened the rear door directly behind the driver's seat. She undid first one child seat, then the other, her fingers moving mechanically; she'd done this a thousand times.

Life was funny. At eighteen, when she'd imagined herself at thirty, she would have thought that she would be at least half a continent away from both her mother and from Hades. She'd wanted to do something different, something important with her life.

Instead, hers had turned out to be a very old story, almost as old as time itself. Nursing a crush from the time she was ten, she had fallen under the spell of a handsome local one fateful night. Leading with her heart instead of the brains that God had given her, she had one wonderful experience and then very quickly found herself pregnant. With no one to turn to, she was trying to work up her nerve to tell the man who had captured her heart that he was about to be a father when she discovered that he'd abruptly left town. Leaving her emotionally stranded.

Not that he had done any of this on purpose. He had no more clue that she was pregnant than her mother did. It wasn't as if they'd been going together before that night. They had run into each other, she walking off the effects of another awful argument with her mother and he coming back from a trip to Anchorage. She was walking along the road by the lake, and he'd slowed down his car to ask her if she wanted a drive home.

Home was the last place she'd wanted to go and said so. But he hadn't wanted to leave her alone out there, so he offered to keep her company. They'd sat in his car and talked. About his plans. About hers. And then, somehow, magic had happened. Magic that had nothing to do with her mother or the woman he was supposedly engaged to, or the woman he'd been writing to who he'd invited to come out here to live. It was the first time she'd ever seen him looking anything but decisive. But he was having doubts about the future.

They both took shelter in the present. In the moment. In each other.

And soon after that, he left Hades. Left because Lila Montgomery had changed her mind. Lila Montgomery who'd once bragged that she could have any man. And she had wanted Ben.

Opening her front door, Heather realized that Ben had never answered the question she'd asked him at the clinic. He never said what he was doing back. Or how long he intended on staying. Was this just a visit or the beginning of something permanent?

She had no idea which she was rooting for.

Shepherding the girls in front of her, Heather entered the house. "Mother, we're back."

She heard the floorboards creak as the wheelchair slid over them.

"Did you remember to pick up my medication?"

Martha demanded sharply as she propelled her wheelchair into the room.

Heather felt her stomach drop another notch.

Chapter Four

Please, please, let me get out of here without an argument.

Mindful that the girls would pick up any exchange of heated words, Heather hoped her mother would just drop the matter, even though she knew better. Martha Ryan let nothing drop until she was good and ready.

One hand on each little girl, Heather shepherded them toward the kitchen. She'd left snacks for them in the refrigerator.

"Sorry." She tossed the apology over her shoulder. "I'll pick it up on my way home."

Heather didn't have to look to know that her mother was glaring at her. She could feel it.

"If you don't forget."

Heather kept her voice upbeat and cheerful. "I won't forget."

"You forgot this morning," her mother accused.

"I was in a hurry," Heather pointed out.

It wasn't easy keeping the irritation and frustration out of her voice. She certainly hadn't forgotten her mother's medication on purpose. Seeing Ben had knocked every thought out of her head. Besides, it wasn't as if her mother was down to her last dose. There was enough for several more days. And yet, forgetting the medication was just another "failing" to upbraid her for. Her mother never cut her any slack. She'd even taken her to task for some minor oversight the day of Joe's funeral.

"And tonight you'll be tired," Martha declared as if it was a foregone conclusion.

"I'll go and pick your medicine up during my lunch break." She saw her mother open her mouth for another go-round. Sometimes she thought that the woman lived for arguments. "Mother, I have to go."

Heather deliberately turned her back on her mother, hoping that was the end of it. Bending down, she kissed first one girl and then the other. She didn't think she would have been able to stand it if they weren't in her life. Hannah and Hayley were what kept her going. What kept her sane.

She hugged them both quickly. "You two be good today and be sure to help your grandmother, okay?"

Hannah made no protest. She merely nodded as a little sigh escaped her lips. In many ways, Hannah was more like her than Hayley was.

"Okay."

Hayley appeared far less bound to the request, even though she made no protest. Instead, she shrugged her small shoulders and Heather had the impression that her daughter was flinching off the request with the same minute motion.

"Sure, Mama."

"That's my girls." Heather smiled at her daughters. She rose and slid the straps of her purse back up onto her shoulder, then headed toward the front door. "See you tonight."

"How's their rash?" The question came across like a demand for information as Martha propelled her wheelchair, following Heather into the living room.

"Gone." Heather hoped the one-word answer would satisfy her mother. She should have known better.

Martha made a disparaging noise. "I could have told you that and saved you some money."

"Shayne didn't charge me."

"That's probably because he overcharged you to begin with."

Heather struggled with a flash of temper, which happened more frequently the longer she took care of her mother. Knowing it would lead to an exchange of words she didn't want her girls overhearing, Heather banked it down.

"He didn't overcharge me to begin with, Mother." Her tone turned frosty. She hated that her mother turned her into a person who was less than compassionate, less than kind. She didn't like to think she could be stripped of these traits, but her mother always sapped everything out of her. "I'll see you tonight." Looking back toward the kitchen, she raised her voice so that her daughters could hear. "Bye, pumpkins."

To her surprise, just as she turned to make her escape, her mother caught her arm. "What's wrong?"

She refused to believe that her mother could see through her. That would take some sort of bond, some sort of connection, and they had never had one. "I'm going to be late, Mother, that's what's wrong."

But Martha continued to hold on to her wrist, apparently not satisfied with the answer. "You're shaking."

Heather extricated her wrist from her mother's grasp. She needed to get to work and get a grip. Her mother prevented her from doing both.

"Not enough sleep last night," she lied, hoping that would be the end of it.

"What do you have to keep you awake at night?" Martha asked. "You're not the one who's stuck in a chair, looking up at people all the time. The object of everyone's pity."

Heather was tired of being made to feel guilty for something that had never been her fault. And if she stopped to give her mother a pep talk, the way she had countless times before, she would make herself late.

"No, I'm not, Mother. But I have to go to work. We can discuss this later." And with that, she hurried out the door, closing it quickly behind her. She could still hear her mother's voice as she went down the porch steps.

With effort, Heather found she could block out the words, if not the sound.

She knew that part of her mother's bitterness stemmed from being felled by myasthenia gravis, the disease that rendered her legs nearly useless. Heather couldn't help feeling guilty at wanting to escape, guilty because she hadn't the time or the in- clination to remain a few extra minutes, trying to placate the woman. Her mother was not to be coaxed out of that dark place this morning. There were times, like today, when her mother seemed to enjoy wallowing in self-pity.

Once in her car, Heather started it up and backed away from the house. She hated leaving her girls to witness this. But school was out for the summer and the day care center that Shayne's wife ordinarily ran was closed this week. Sydney was taking a well- deserved rest, and Heather could hardly blame her. At the same time, it did make things very difficult for her.

She hated asking her mother for favors, any kind of favor. And her mother had grumbled when she'd asked her to keep an eye on the girls this week. One would think that she'd welcome the company instead of remaining alone the way she normally did for a good part of each day.

Heather sighed. She'd given up trying to figure her mother out. Not to mention trying to brighten the woman's life as best she could. Some people preferred living inside a cave, enveloped by darkness. Her mother was one of those people.

It was only going to get worse.

Heather pressed her lips together. She did not look forward to her mother learning about Ben's return. Martha Ryan had never had a good word to say about him. Ben's charm left her cold, perhaps because it reminded her so much of her own husband.

Though she'd idolized her father, Heather couldn't remember John Ryan ever being nearly as charming as Ben. Or as intelligent, for that matter. Ben didn't have just street smarts, he had a mind that quite simply left others, including his own brother's, in the dust. He always seemed to absorb things more easily and quickly. That was why at the age where other students were just graduating college, Ben was graduating from medical school. It had never even occurred to him that he had done anything out of the ordinary.

She sighed as she came to a stop at Hades's only traffic light. There she went, being his advocate. Why? He didn't need her taking up his cause, even silently. The very last thing she needed right now was to clutter up her mind with thoughts of Ben. She was years beyond that young girl with the hopeless crush. The girl whose very breath stopped in her lungs whenever he looked in her direction. That had been an entire lifetime ago.

She and Ben had nothing in common now.

Nothing but Hannah, she thought.

Except that Ben didn't know about that. No one did, not even Shayne, who'd delivered her baby.

Finding herself pregnant had been the scariest period of her life. And then Joe Kendall had come to the rescue. Poor, dear Joe, her lumbering giant who had loved her with the complete devotion of a puppy. Who'd told her that he would work and slave to provide for her, pledging the rest of his life and undying love if only she would agree to marry him.

So she had. What choice did she have, really? Hades was not a condemning community, but being an unwed mother was a stigma she wasn't willing to endure if she could avoid it. She especially didn't want her baby coming into the world without a father's name.

And even if no one ever said a word to her about it, never even appeared to give it a second thought, she knew that her mother would make her life miserable because of her momentary transgression. Worse, her mother would make the life of her unborn child miserable. So she had said yes to Joe and silently vowed to be the best wife she could.

For a while, their marriage had gone well. Joe gave no indication he ever suspected that Hannah wasn't his. And when Hayley came along, exploding like a fire cracker almost from the moment she was born, Joe had been beside himself with joy.

Heather eased her car toward the north side of town. She could still remember the look in Joe's eyes when he told her how happy he was. And how grateful he was to her for it.

That was the night before the cave-in.

At least he died thinking she loved him. And in her own way, she had. But she had loved Joe the way she would have loved a beloved friend.

Not the way she had loved Ben.

Ben she had loved with all her young heart. So much so that whenever she was near him, she was positive he could somehow feel that love all but overflowing her veins. Washing over him. She was certain of it that night at the lake. Certain that he somehow knew, sensed, what she couldn't tell him: how she loved him, and how they were meant to be together.

But that had turned out to be a sophomoric delusion. She was acutely aware of this a little more than three weeks later, when she'd heard that not only was Ben not there to greet the woman he'd proposed marriage to in his letters, but that he had run off with someone she felt in her heart didn't really love him.

Moot, all moot, she told herself as she saw the restaurant come into view.

There was no reason for her to dwell on any of this. It was in her past. And soon Ben would be in her past again. The man would be gone before she knew it. Hades was far too small to contain him. He didn't have his brother's temperament. He might have been smarter than Shayne, but he didn't possess Shayne's compassion. And that was what you needed to remain here, to practice medicine and earn rewards that were not tangible: compassion.

No, Ben wasn't meant to remain long in Hades. She just had to find a way to get through the days until he left again.

A hollow feeling wove through her, even though she knew his departure was inevitable. It was also for the best.

After parking her ten-year-old car, kept alive through faith and June Yearling Quintano's almost magical mechanical abilities, Heather got out and hurried into the restaurant.

The parking lot was empty. She'd just managed to miss the early breakfast crowd. Just as well. She still needed a little time to pull herself together.

Lily Quintano Yearling looked up the moment she walked into the small, homey restaurant. Her smile was warm, genuine. Still a workaholic, life in Hades had managed to unfurrow Lily's brow and forced her to appreciate the journey as well as the goal.

"I thought you weren't coming in until after nine or so."

For many of the miners and especially the gaggle of unattached bachelors who populated Hades, Lily's was a second home, the place where they ate not just an occasional meal but all of them. Her cooking brought memories of their upbringing back to them—if their mother had been a gourmet chef with a knack for turning even the most common of meals into a treat for the palate.

"I got lucky," Heather told her, shrugging out of her sweater. "I was at the clinic with the girls when they opened up this morning."

Pausing to straighten a tablecloth that had been put out only minutes ago, Lily asked, "How are they doing?"

"They're all better."

Thank God, Heather added silently. When the girls had first come down with the rash, she'd been afraid of complications. Or, at the very least, scarring. But the ugly blemishes had disappeared without a trace.

Lily shook her head as she crossed the room. "I don't know how you do it, Heather. You take care of the girls, who are clearly a handful, you're there for your mother and still you manage to work full-time."

To her it was just a matter of putting one foot in front of the other, getting through the day. But she had to admit, this was not the way she'd seen her life going when she was in high school. Back then she'd had dreams of going to college, of developing her artistic abilities and making something of herself.

The world had held promise. Now it held bills with due dates on them.

"You do what you have to," Heather told her. And then she smiled as she looked at the slightly rounded bulge that existed where once Lily's flat stomach had been. The baby, Lily's first, was due in four months. "You'll find out soon enough." Her smile widened, reaching her eyes. "I've got a feeling that nothing will ever make you stay at home to be a full-time mother."

Lily had never been in the position that Heather found herself in. For a good part of her life, her older brother, Kevin, had looked after her and her siblings. And now she had a husband beside her.

"Yes, but I don't have a mother to care for and I won't be facing motherhood alone." Lily bit her tongue, as if chagrined. "Sorry, didn't mean that the way it came out. Max says I've still got a long way to go before I'm not so outspoken."

Once she stored her purse inside the hostess desk, Heather took out her small apron and tied it around her waist. She dismissed the apology. "Nothing wrong with honesty."

"Unless it comes with a razor tongue," Max qualified, coming up behind his wife. Slipping his arms around her waist, the sheriff of Hades paused for a second to nuzzle Lily before declaring his intentions. He nodded a greeting at Heather. "Now that reinforcements are here, I've got to go back to keeping the streets of Hades safe."

He moved his hands along her belly for a moment before he made his way around the table. "Take care of the little guy."

"Girl," Lily countered, placing her hand protectively over the tiny bump in her midsection.

Leaning over the table, he kissed her. "We'll see."

Heather couldn't help feeling a little wistful as she watched the exchange. She waited until Max crossed to the front door and exited. "He's really looking forward to being a father, isn't he?"

"Champing at the bit," Lily agreed. "Between Max and his grandmother," she said, referring to Hades's very lively postmistress, Ursula Hatcher, who had just recently taken a fourth husband to her bed, "I don't think I'm going to get a chance to hold this baby before she or he graduates high school." Ursula looked in on her at least once a day to monitor her progress. "Thank God June's going to give birth first." June was her husband's younger sister, who had recently bought back her old auto-repair shop at her new husband's suggestion. The latter also happened to be Lily's older brother, Kevin. "It's my only hope," she added with a grin.

And then, just like that, as if a cloud had suddenly passed in front of the sun, her smile faded. Lily paled.

A veteran of the silent battle being waged, Heather recognized the signs immediately. "Morning sickness back?"

Lily seemed to struggle. "It never left."

Sympathy flooded her. Heather shooed her boss away. "Go," she ordered. "I'll man the fort." Placing her hands to Lily's back, she sent the older woman toward the alcove where the two restrooms were located.

"To do that, wouldn't you have to be a man?"

The low voice that asked the question rippled over Heather's skin even before she turned around to look toward the doorway. With the exception of this morning, she hadn't heard Ben's baritone voice in seven years. And yet, it seemed to be imprinted on her brain.

"Sometimes you need to improvise." Forcing a smile to her lips, Heather turned to look at him. He wasn't wearing the white lab coat. Had he tired of being a doctor already? "What can I do for you?"

"It's more like what I can do for you." The smile that graced his face went straight to her gut like a well-aimed shot.

"Oh?"

Breathe, Heather, *breathe,* she ordered herself. The air in her lungs refused to circulate. It became a solid entity while her pulse raced like a car in the Indianapolis 500.

"Your mother called the clinic."

"Oh."

The news did not surprise her. Her mother often called ahead before she had a chance to arrive, as if she didn't think her capable of remembering what needed to be done. Forgetting her medication this morning only reinforced her mother's belief that she was generally incompetent.

"She said you forgot to pick up her medicine and to please have someone bring it over to you because you're liable to forget it again." Amusement sparked in his eyes as he told her about the call. Her mother's telephone manners were no better than her manners in general. Undoubtedly, the woman had gone on to complain about her.

Embarrassed, Heather flushed. "Sorry about that."

His smile only widened. He produced the bag with the medication inside and placed it on the table before her. "No problem. Shayne said to tell you it was being put on her account."

She started to reach for the bag until a thought occurred to her. Her eyes met his. "Um, who did my mother speak to?"

"Me." He tried to keep a straight face but failed. "You know, your mother has a great future in interrogation if she ever wants to start a new career."

Mortified, Heather found herself wishing that the ground would open up and swallow her. She wasn't even aware of murmuring, "Oh, God." But she *was* aware that her mother now knew Ben was back in Hades. And that there would be a host of questions when she went home tonight.

Chapter Five

Heather could just hear the questions her mother must have fired at Ben once she realized that he was back in Hades. She was surprised he had actually been able to break away in order to come here. Or that he had been willing to bring over the medication after the interrogation.

"I apologize."

He looked as if he wasn't sure what to make of her words. "For what?"

"My mother."

Heather moved around the small, homey restaurant, wishing for people to wait on. Usually at least a few stragglers came after breakfast, men who were in no hurry to get anywhere. But today there were only sunbeams there. No one to divert her attention from him.

Trouble was, even after all this time, raising her eyes toward him also managed to raise her body temperature several degrees.

"My mother has a tendency to be a little abrupt and say the first thing that comes to her mind." Which was putting it mildly. But calling her mother rude wasn't something she was inclined to do except within the recesses of her own mind. Embarrassed, she wanted to make it up to him somehow.

All she had to work with was food. She looked at him ruefully. "Would you like a cup of coffee?"

Ben smiled. "Trying to make amends?"

She flushed, but she would have to be dead not to respond to his smile. "Yes."

He laughed, shaking his head. Martha Ryan had been caustic and sarcastic in her questions about his return. But Heather wasn't to blame for her mother's behavior. He didn't want her thinking that he held her accountable for Martha in any way.

"I'd like some coffee," he told her, "but only if you'll let me pay for it." He placed a bill on the table between them. "To go," Ben qualified. "I told Shayne I'd be right back. I don't want him thinking that I've disappeared my first day at work."

Heather nodded. "I'll see what I can do."

Unlike at the lunch counter in the back of The General Store, or Ike and Luc's Salty Dog Saloon where food to go was a common enough occurrence, Lily's was considered a sit-down restaurant, somewhere that a person could carve out a few minutes of peace, either exclusively for themselves or with someone else. The idea was to enjoy a meal away from the hustle of the everyday world.

But in order to accommodate her customers on those rare occasions when they couldn't finish a meal, Lily kept foam containers on hand for both food and beverages. Heather tried to remember where they were kept as she walked into the kitchen.

It took her only a second to become aware that she wasn't alone. Her pulse rate had gone up again.

"I'll bring it to you," she promised. Opening the overhead cabinets, she discovered the cups and lids on her third try.

When she glanced at him over her shoulder, Heather found herself getting caught up in his engaging grin. It took effort to look away. If this kept up, her body would rival the consistency of two-day old pudding.

"I don't mind coming in here," he told her. "It gives me an extra couple of minutes to talk to you."

Why would he want to do that? And then Heather stiffened as the reason occurred to her.

Had Ben figured it out? Back at the clinic, when he'd looked down into Hannah's face, had he seen traces of himself in the little girl's features? He could have easily looked up Hannah's age in her chart and done the math. The possibility was right there, it didn't take a genius to see it.

Her tongue was so dry, she had trouble getting the words out. "About what?"

He began to say something, but her expression stopped him. "You've got that look on your face."

She had never been able to maintain a blank expression. All her thoughts, all her feelings, had always been right out there for the world to see. She would have made a lousy spy, Heather thought ruefully. One look at her face would have told the enemy everything.

But she tried her best to feign innocence. "What look?"

"The one that people get when they're facing an IRS audit and all their papers to back up their entries were destroyed in a fire two days ago."

She lifted one shoulder in a dismissive shrug and avoided making eye contact. "Sorry, just a little tense."

Ben thought of the all-but-one-sided conversation he'd just had before coming over to the restaurant. "Your mother live with you?"

"After she came down with myasthenia gravis, Joe built a house for her on our property. Just a tiny guest house, really," she explained. Although by no stretch of the imagination was her mother ever a guest, Heather added silently. "But for the most part my mother stays in the main house." They had a guest room on the first floor. She'd wanted to make it into a playroom for the girls but her mother had commandeered it right after Joe died. "So yes, I suppose you could say that she lives with me."

That would explain a lot, Ben thought. He'd looked up Martha Ryan's medical folder after she'd called the clinic just to familiarize himself with her condition. The burden of the disease she'd contracted had soured more than its share of people, and as he recalled, Martha Ryan hadn't had a sunny disposition to begin with.

No wonder Heather looked like a cat on a hot tin roof. A beautiful cat. But he wasn't supposed to think like that anymore, he reminded himself, not if he wanted to prove to Shayne that he was serious.

Though there was no one else in the restaurant, he leaned forward and said, "You've got a lot on your shoulders."

Was that admiration in his voice? She tried desperately not to pay attention, especially to how his breath grazed her cheek and goose bumps sprang up to mark its path.

She cleared her throat. "Nothing more than what a lot of other people have to deal with."

She was being modest, but then, if he recalled correctly, Heather always had a penchant for being modest, retiring. Which was why he'd been so surprised with the intensity of her lovemaking that single night at the lake.

Still waters ran deep.

He'd always thought that, looking into her eyes.

"Being sole supporter of two little girls and an invalid mother isn't exactly something most people have to deal with, especially not at twenty-nine."

"I'm thirty," she corrected.

"Oh, well, that makes a difference. Thirty," he repeated. "That puts you with almost one foot in the grave."

At times she felt like that. Worn-out and old before her years, especially after a go-round with her mother. But to hear Ben say it, especially with that little smile of his lighting up everything within a ten-mile radius, Heather could feel humor bubbling up inside her. Could laugh at her own seriousness.

Could feel his light drifting into her very being.

She pushed that down. This wasn't seven years ago. "You take it black?"

"Life?" His eyes held hers as he moved his head from side to side. "No. I generally take it with a ray of sunshine."

She pressed her lips together to hold back her grin. "The coffee."

This time he inclined his head. "As black as you can get it."

Heather had always liked her coffee a pleasant shade of light brown, made that way with an ocean of cream and a forklift full of sugar. She could never understand how some people preferred their coffee to have the consistency of asphalt.

"Alfred was retarring the parking lot behind the restaurant last week," she said, referring to the local handyman. "I could check to see if there might be some left."

His eyes shifted to the pot of coffee she picked up. "No, that'll do fine."

He was smiling again. Smiling right at her. A shower of lights rained over her, bringing with it an almost overwhelming warmth that enveloped her so tightly it was hard for her to catch her breath. Taking the foam cup in her hand, she filled it to the brim with coffee, grateful she hadn't spilled any over the top.

"So, how have you been?"

Setting down the coffeepot, she took a lid and sealed the cup. "Since I left the clinic this morning?" Done, Heather held the cup out to him. "Or since you left Hades?"

A bemused smile played along his lips as he watched her. She knew he was trying to figure out what she was talking about. That made two of them, she thought. "The latter."

"Okay." Like a marathon runner taking off at the sound of the starter pistol, she rattled off the events of her life in the past seven years. They squeezed themselves into a very small space. "I got married, had two kids, was widowed and started working here." Taking a breath, she forced herself to meet his eyes. "Not exactly something to turn into the movie of the week."

The tempo of her pulse picked up again but she refused to look away. She didn't want him thinking that she was avoiding him. The last thing in the world she needed was for him to connect the dots of her life and realize that he'd left more than just his impression on her that fateful night.

After she'd dealt with the shock of finding out that she was pregnant and the sobering news that she had no one to turn to, she'd made up her mind that Ben would never find out that he was Hannah's father.

Heather was determined to take care of her daughters, and she didn't need anyone feeling sorry for her. She needed a few good breaks. The most important had come in the guise of Alison's sister, Lily. When Lily had offered her work that afternoon at Joe's wake—a wake that Lily had catered and refused to accept any money for—it was all she could do to keep from crying. She'd accepted the second the words had been out of Lily's mouth.

"You're the one with the exciting life," she said, hoping to divert his attention to a more favorable topic.

Ben laughed softly to himself. "Not if you see it from this end."

Heather looked carefully at the man who had stolen her heart so long ago. It occurred to her that perhaps his life hadn't been quite as carefree as she'd assumed.

"I'm sorry about you and Lila." When Ben raised a quizzical eyebrow at her words, she could feel her tongue thickening in her mouth. "I mean, I just assumed that things didn't turn out. She's not here with you." Again Heather realized she was making assumptions that could be completely wrong. "I mean, she's not, is she?"

She bit her lower lip. "Look, I've got a lot to do—"

Bambi caught in headlights had looked more serene. Why was she reacting this way to him? "Do I make you nervous, Heather?"

"No." The denial instantly sprang to her lips. But she'd never been very good at lying. "Yes," she admitted. How hopelessly stupid that must sound to him. She shrugged, looking away. Wishing that some enterprising scientist had invented shots against sounding like a hayseed. "I don't know."

This time, the soft laugh was hers exclusively. "It's been a long time since I came across a multiple-choice answer." And then he gazed into her eyes. Creating tidal waves around her navel. "I don't mean to make you nervous, Heather."

He would have to stop breathing for that, she thought. And leave town again. For good. But because he was being so nice about the fact that she kept alternating feet and shoving them into her mouth, Heather shook her head at his words.

"You're not making me nervous," she lied. "It hasn't been one of my better mornings, and I guess I'm just a little surprised to see you back, that's all."

He grinned, and the corners of his eyes crinkled.

And she melted a little more. "Not half as surprised as Shayne was last night."

"He didn't know you were coming back, either?"

Ben liked the way her eyes widened when she looked surprised. They were a beautiful shade of blue.

"Heather, I didn't even know I was coming back. Not until this last week."

Compassion flooded through her. "Was that when she left you?" She backtracked again. "I mean, assuming she left you."

He supposed he could have lied to save his ego. But somehow, it didn't seem right, lying to someone who was so completely honest, so guileless. Besides, the story would be out soon enough. Ursula would see to that. The seventy-plus-year-old postmistress dispensed local news along with the mail like clockwork.

So he nodded. "She left me."

It was, at bottom, despite her initial assumption, a difficult thing for her to fathom, much less absorb. "I really never thought that kind of thing could happen to you."

He supposed that was how mortals learned humility. He'd certainly gotten a huge dose of it. It made him reevaluate everything about his life, about his past and the path of his future.

"Join the club." His tone was self-disparaging.

She'd never liked Lila, Heather thought. Never liked the woman for taking Ben away and liked her even less for hurting him.

"So you came back here to pull yourself together?"

"Something like that," he allowed, then heard himself adding, "Actually, Lila's been gone for a year. I came back to Hades to make amends. And because Hades is my home."

It wasn't something he would have ordinarily admitted, but he liked talking to Heather. He'd always had the gift of gab, which he'd used to charm, to beguile and to get himself out of a jam. Never to share a thought, a feeling, for its own sake. He found doing so intriguing.

"Thinking that if you did that, if you made amends, maybe things would straighten out in your life, the universe would smile on you again and that Lila would come back to you?"

"You read tea leaves, too?"

"No." She shrugged carelessly, not wanting him to think she was trying to be clever. "Just been down that path, that's all," Heather admitted. "Making deals with God, thinking that if I did things just so, everything would fall into place, would follow an order and make things happen the way I wanted them to."

For a second it was almost as if they were sharing a single thought. He shook his head, seeing the humor in the effort. "Didn't work for you, I take it?"

Heather wondered what he would say if he knew that she had prayed for him.

"Can't complain," she said.

"No, you never did," he recalled.

"How would you know that?"

"It's not that big a town, Heather." He thought of Ursula. "Everyone knows everything about everyone."

She thought of Hannah. Thank God, he was wrong. "Not always."

Because Hannah had been such a tiny baby, everyone thought she had been born prematurely instead of at full term. Had Hannah been a big baby, people might have been tempted to count backward on their fingers and either assume she and Joe had consummated their union before ever taking their vows, or quietly speculate about Hannah's true paternity.

He grinned. "You're being very mysterious."

For once she didn't blush or dismiss her own words. "No one can really know what's in another person's heart or mind," she told him. "Not if that person doesn't want you to."

"Why, Heather, what kind of secrets are you hiding?" he teased, moving just a shade closer to her.

Nothing I can share with you. Heather glanced at her watch. Lily had been gone this entire time. "I'd better go check on Lily."

Lily. The name that was written across the front of the restaurant, belonging to a woman he'd never met. Funny how he'd just assumed that he would find Hades exactly the way he'd left it, with everyone exactly as he'd left them.

Instead, his brother had married and he was still adjusting to the fact that rather than lose personnel, the clinic had gained people. When he'd left, besides Shayne there'd been a nurse working there who had also doubled as a midwife. Edna Carter was at least seventy-five and probably ten years older than that. She'd retired and gone to live with her daughter in Hawaii the week before he'd run off with Lila.

That had been the natural course of things. People left Hades, they didn't come to it, much less remain. Yet two new people worked at the clinic and another new person ran a restaurant. Civilization had finally appeared in their tiny hamlet.

"What's wrong with Lily?" he asked.

"She's pregnant. Four months along," she explained. "Lily's married to Max."

Now there was a name he recognized. And the information stunned him. "Max Yearling?" he asked, even though there'd only been one Max in Hades when he'd left. "The sheriff?" he qualified when she nodded. He'd had the impression that Max was one of those rare, self-contained men who needed little in the way of companionship, certainly not a wife. "Max got married?"

"To Alison's sister. Alison LeBlanc," she added in case he'd gotten lost. "The nurse-practitioner at the clinic. She's Luc's wife."

He'd just made her acquaintance a couple of minutes before he'd come to see Heather with the medicine. "Luc? Jean Luc?"

She liked being the source of information. It gave her an odd sense of control, something that tended to elude her during the normal course of her daily life. "Ike's married, too. To Sydney's friend, Marta."

She was pulling his leg now, he thought. But she'd gone too far. "Not Ike." Ike liked the ladies too much. "He said he'd never get married."

"He lied," she laughed. "You've got a lot of catching up to do."

"Apparently." He paused, looking at her. Despite what she'd gone through, the years had been kind to her. She was more beautiful than he remembered. "Want to help me?"

Her playful tone vanished. "Excuse me?"

"Catch up," he clarified. "Tonight, after the clinic closes up."

Panic slipped in, wearing boots. "I have to go home. The girls—"

He had an even better idea. "Why don't I take you and the girls out to dinner?"

She pointed out the obvious, something that might have escaped him in his time away. "This is the only place that doesn't serve dinner on a chipped plate," she told him. "Other than at my house."

He grinned at her, turning her mental processes to mush. "Are you inviting me over?"

"No. I mean—" She took a breath, trying to steady her pulse. "This is a little short notice."

He cocked his head, summoning an innocent look. "Are you going to make me beg?"

She didn't want him thinking she was being coy. "No, it's just that—"

"I'll be on my best behavior," he promised, crossing his heart.

You had me at hello, she thought. Except that there were more people than just her involved. "It's not that, it's just that my mother—"

"Why don't you let me worry about your mother?" he suggested easily. "If I'm going to be a doctor here, it's time I started mending a few fences."

"Maybe you should start with something a little less taxing than my mother."

"I always liked a challenge."

She shook her head. She'd thought he would have realized what he was up against after her mother's call. "A challenge is going over Niagara Falls in a barrel. Dealing with my mother is like throwing yourself off the Empire State Building—without a parachute. Even King Kong couldn't survive."

He laughed. "Then we'll go back to my original suggestion. Dinner here. You, the girls and me."

Heather bit back her protest. The girls loved going out to eat. And she had to admit, being here with Ben was preferable to going home and listening to her mother give her the third degree about her day—and him.

"Dinner here," she echoed.

He took that as a yes. "What time?"

She got off at five, but she needed some time to get the girls and herself ready. "Seven."

He nodded. "Works for me."

That's what he said now...Heather could only pray that he wouldn't be regretting his words by evening's end.

The next moment, she remembered that she still hadn't attended to Lily. "Oh, God, Lily!"

"Need help?" he offered.

"No," she said over her shoulder as she quickly hurried off to the restroom. Throwing up while pregnant was a girl thing. Men were not a welcome audience. Not even if they were good-looking doctors.

Chapter Six

Heather entered the small, brightly decorated restroom with its soft-mother-of-pearl-pink tiles. Lily was leaning over the sink, her knuckles pressed against the countertop. Even with the benefit of three halogen lights in the ceiling, her complexion looked incredibly pale.

"Lily, it's been at least ten minutes. Do you want me to get a doctor?"

"No. I'm okay. I'm okay," Lily repeated, as if saying the phrase twice would make it so. The horrible wave of nausea temporarily abating, Lily had thrown cold water in her face in the hopes of appearing a little more robust than death warmed over.

Heather watched her closely. Her boss didn't seem okay, no matter how much she protested. It wasn't her place to tell Lily what to do, but right now she wasn't speaking as an employee. This was a conversation between two women touched by life's greatest miracle. A miracle that sometimes came with one hell of an upset stomach.

"Maybe you should think about taking a few days off, Lily?" she suggested. "This won't last forever."

Lily forced a smile to her lips, waiting for the next wave to hit. "If it keeps up like this, neither will I." She drew in a tentative breath. Her eyes met Heather's. "If I'm not here, who'll do the cooking?"

There were three of them to wait on the customers, but only one chef and that was Lily. Six days a week found her here from the moment the doors opened at seven until they closed again at ten. She knew that Max was pushing for her to hire help, but so far, perfectionist that she was, Lily had remained firm.

Heather drew her courage to her. "I could. It wouldn't be as good as your cooking," she added quickly, "but the customers wouldn't be poisoned. And Lily's would stay open."

"Lily *needs* to work." She referred to herself in the third person whimsically because hers was the name on the outside of the restaurant. "But, thanks. I do appreciate the offer and I'll keep it in mind if I get any worse," she promised.

Walking out of the restroom first, Lily collided

with a tall man she didn't recognize. Startled, she took a step back.

"Oh, sorry. I—"

Ben had decided to hang around just in case he *was* needed. The woman looked a little peaked, but otherwise showed no indication of physical distress. He raised his eyes toward Heather, who was directly behind the other woman. He had only one question.

"Lily?" he asked.

"Lily," Heather confirmed.

The woman narrowed her eyes. "And you are?"

Ben inclined his head. The smile on his face flowered. The word *irresistible* flashed through Heather's mind. Nothing had changed. Ben had only become more so in the last seven years. God help the female population of the world. And her.

"Dr. Benjamin David Kerrigan," he told Lily.

Seeing the puzzled expression on Lily's face, Heather interjected, "Ben is Shayne's younger brother."

Lily glanced from the tall man to Heather. "Shayne never mentioned having a brother."

Ben laughed softly. That was Shayne, close-mouthed to a fault. No one ever knew when something was bothering his older brother. He wondered if Shayne had ever opened up to his wife, or if she found that trait as frustrating as he had when they were growing up.

"No, I don't suspect that he would have," Ben said easily. "We weren't on the best of terms when

I left town." He glanced at Heather to see if she had any contradictions to offer regarding the way he'd departed from Hades. But she said nothing. He turned again to the short, dark-haired woman in front of him. Her abdomen was almost as flat as an ironing board. But that meant nothing. Women who were pregnant showed at different times, especially when it was their first child. "How far along are you?"

"Almost five months." Lily placed her hand on the slight swell. She'd been counting on Shayne to deliver her baby. Jimmy was a very good doctor, but he was a heart specialist. Besides, he was her younger brother and unless she was marooned somewhere on an ice floe, she would have rather not have him deliver her baby. "Is Shayne leaving Hades?"

Ben grinned. "Shayne would have to be surgically excised to leave Hades. I've just come to join his practice," he explained. "I figure there are enough sick people to go around." Ben looked at her thoughtfully. From the looks of it, her pregnancy had been pretty miserable. There were circles beneath her otherwise very attractive eyes. "Try sprinkling ginger on your food."

"Ginger?" Lily echoed, wondering if she'd heard him correctly.

He nodded. "It's a spice. I could ask Mrs. Kellogg at The Emporium to order it—"

"It's called The General Store now," Heather told him. "Luc and Ike bought it."

"The General Store, then. You could still—"

Lily drew herself up to her full short height. "I know what ginger is," she informed him. "But how will that—"

"It just will," he assured her with a look that Heather had often thought was capable of selling an icemaker to every Inuit in the area over the age of two.

Lily drew in a breath. "Okay," she said with a sigh. "Ginger it is. Right about now, I'd be willing to do a rain dance naked in the center of town if that meant I'd stop being so damn nauseous all the time."

"A naked rain dance," Ben repeated thoughtfully, suppressing a grin. "Now, there's an approach I hadn't heard of. But I'd try the ginger first if I were you." He had to be going. Shayne would start thinking that he'd left town again if he didn't show up soon. Before reaching the front entrance with his container of coffee, he nodded at Heather. "I'll see you later tonight."

"Tonight," Heather echoed, her mouth suddenly as dry as sand. What was worse, her knees had suddenly locked.

There was more than just mild interest in Lily's eyes. "Old friend?"

The last thing she wanted to do was answer personal questions about Ben. Lowering her eyes to avoid Lily's penetrating gaze, Heather murmured, "Something like that."

"Oh."

The single word caught her attention. She looked at Lily sharply. "What do you mean 'oh'?"

"Just that. Oh." A knowing smile bloomed on Lily's lips. But before she could say anything further, the front door opened. "I'll be right back," Lily promised, moving toward the back stairs. "I'm going down to check the storeroom to see how much ginger we have on hand."

Lily obviously assumed that there was something between her and Ben. Well, there was, but not what anyone would ever guess, Heather thought as she walked to the front of the restaurant.

She was surprised to see Hades's postmistress, Ursula, making her way to the hostess desk.

Ordinarily, Ursula only came to Lily's to take part in some celebration. The people in Hades often gathered together for a party, using any excuse to celebrate. Lily's caught the more family-oriented ones while Ike's Salty Dog Saloon was the site of all the others. Births, weddings, comings and goings were all reasons to tip back a few beers and unwind in the company of the immediate town.

But this was still the breakfast hour and she couldn't recall ever seeing Ursula here by herself.

Putting on her most inviting smile, Heather greeted the woman. "Good morning, Mrs.—"

Stunned, Heather realized that she had gone blank as to which last name she needed to use in order to address the woman. Known generally as Ursula Hatcher, the bawdy postmistress had been married a total of four times, having buried three very contented husbands before she'd married her present one, a strong, wiry miner named Yuri. It was Yuri's very Russian last name that escaped her.

"Ursula," the postmistress said in her deep, booming voice. "I keep telling you to call me Ursula." She gave Heather a wide grin. "You're old enough to do that now, and Lord knows my last name keeps changing often enough to confuse even the local preacher." She lowered her voice slightly, as if letting Heather in on a secret. "I actually thought about not changing it this time around, just leaving it at Hatcher, but of course that hurt Yuri's pride."

She rolled her eyes, the gesture saying "Men" in a tolerant, silent voice. "For some reason, that made him think that I had second thoughts about staying married to him or that I was prejudiced against his people." She laughed, and the sound was more like an infectious cackle. "Isn't that perfectly ridiculous? Given all the time I'd invested in that man…" She shook her head as her voice trailed off for a moment. But then it returned, as deep and booming as ever. "And now I'm Mrs. Barovsky. But that's a mouthful," she attested easily. "So 'Ursula,' though not the prettiest name, is the simplest thing to call me these days." She raised her tufted gray-and-white eyebrows, her eyes gently pinning Heather.

Heather nodded. "All right."

Ursula wasn't sure if her point had gotten across. "All right what?"

Not sure what the woman was after, Heather took a guess. "All right, ma'am?"

"Ma'am?" Ursula echoed incredulously before laughing heartily. "This isn't the army, child. Just Ursula will do."

"All right," Heather repeated. "Ursula," she added the name after a beat.

The exchange earned her another smile as Ursula nodded. "Not bad. You need practice, though." She took a deep breath. "And I need some coffee."

Seeing as how the woman lived directly above the post office where she worked, Heather had no idea why Ursula would make the trip over to Lily's rather than just walk up the stairs to her own living quarters and prepare the coffee there.

The look in Ursula's eyes gave her the uneasy feeling that the older woman could read her thoughts. Her comment almost proved it.

"My coffeemaker's broken. It was slow and Yuri tried to 'improve' it," she chuckled. "Now it won't work at all." Finished with her explanation, she surprised Heather by moving in closer like a conspirator. Ursula lowered her voice to barely audible before asking, "Was that Ben Kerrigan I just saw leaving?"

Heather thought of saying no and hopefully buying Ben a few more hours of privacy. But then she dismissed this as completely idiotic. If he was working at the clinic, news had probably spread. And once Ursula had wind of it, the way she obviously did, no way could his being here be kept under wraps.

Besides, she was no good at lying. Omitting certain truths, yes, but not lying about them. So she gave Ursula the confirmation she was looking for.

"Yes, that was Ben. He came in for coffee, like you. And to drop off my mother's medication." She allowed a sigh to escape her. She should have known better than to raise Ursula's interest. "I forgot it this morning."

"Seeing him this morning threw you for a loop, did it?" Ursula asked in a knowing voice. Smiling, the older woman patted her hand. "Don't worry, honey, your secret's safe with me."

Panic flooded Heather.

"Secret?" she heard herself repeating with a tongue that felt all but numb. "What secret?"

"Why, the crush you had on him, dear. I saw it in your eyes every time you looked his way. Addresses written in illegible handwriting aren't the only thing I can read, child."

There was a long, pregnant pause during which Heather wondered if Ursula suspected something. The woman had always been slightly mysterious, especially in the way she almost always knew when another mine disaster was about to strike—just before it did. It was as if she possessed a sixth sense about some things.

Did the woman know about Hannah?

"Well, I'd better be getting back," Ursula told

her, glancing at her watch. "After I pay for my coffee."

It was a subtle hint to get her moving, Heather realized. As of yet, she hadn't even poured the requested cup of coffee. She hurried into the kitchen to get the pot. After filling the foam container to the top, she carefully sealed the lid.

Handing her a dollar bill, Ursula nodded at the paper bag that Ben had just brought over. "Why don't I just drop that off for you?" The suggestion was tendered innocently. "Your mother might need it."

Her mother disliked visitors. Martha Ryan had vetoed every attempt Heather had made in the last few years to get her together with people, even women her own age.

Heather shook her head. "There's no need for you to trouble yourself, Ursula. Her old medication still hasn't run out."

"No point in waiting to the last minute," Ursula replied cheerfully. "Besides, maybe Martha could use a bit of company." Ursula continued, undaunted.

She appreciated what the woman thought she was doing, but in her mother's case, it was a matter of casting pearls before swine. "I think you're being exceptionally kind, Ursula, but—"

"No 'buts' accepted. Unless, of course, they belong to some young, handsome buck," she added with a mischievous wink. And then she leaned forward so that her voice wouldn't carry beyond a few inches as she whispered, "But don't tell Yuri I said so. He's afraid I might see something I like better and leave him. That's why he insisted we get married. Me, I was enjoying my reputation as a scarlet woman." Her laugh was full-bodied and lusty. "Made for a spicy life." She picked up the container and reached for the bag with Martha's medication. "I'll just take that over to your mother before I head back to the post office."

Reluctantly Heather let her take the bag. "I thought you said you had to be getting back."

"I do." Ursula looked almost as young as her granddaughters when she smiled. "Eventually. April dropped by this morning for a visit. If there's anything that needs my attention immediately, she'll call me." Ursula patted her pocket, then fished out a small silver object for Heather's perusal. "I have a cell phone now. They can find me anywhere, even if I don't want to be found."

At times, Ursula talked so quickly, it was hard to piece everything together. Heather backtracked mentally. "Who is April visiting with?"

Ursula grinned, her eyes sparkling as she replied, "Me."

Heather was tempted to shake her head, if only to clear away the cobwebs. "If she's visiting with you, shouldn't you be there?"

Ursula gave her a very patient look, the kind given to children who proved to be slow. "I will be, dear. Eventually." Crossing to the front door, Ursula paused to look at Heather over her shoulder. "Nice to see Ben back."

She didn't wait for a response.

The restaurant's foot traffic picked up considerably within minutes of Ursula's departure and, much to Heather's relief, remained that way for the rest of the day. Being busy left her no time to think, no time to examine whether or not she was doing the right thing by seeing Ben socially. No time to be nervous about the evening ahead.

When quitting time arrived. Heather was exhausted, and nervousness had set in. She realized her hands were damp and cold. They hadn't felt that way since the day she'd marched down the aisle, about to say "I do" to a lie.

After leaving Lily's, she stopped to take a deep breath. She then slipped behind the steering wheel of her less-than-perfect ten-year-old vehicle. She'd had to give up her Jeep when her mother came to live on the property. The Jeep could not accommodate her mother's wheelchair.

Maybe she should beg off, she thought as she started the car. She could tell Ben that she was too tired to go out tonight.

The next moment she changed her mind. Not because she wasn't tired, but because the effort was doomed to failure. Knowing Ben, he would suggest coming over again, perhaps even with some take-out from the Salty Dog. And that was definitely *not* acceptable, not with her mother lurking around every corner.

She wished she'd had more time to prepare. More time to come up with some kind of viable plan that could get her and the girls out of the house without having to endure an endless game of twenty questions.

Her mouth curved. D-Day would have required less planning and maneuvering.

The attack began the moment she opened the front door and entered.

"Why did that old busybody stop by with my medication?"

It was as if her mother had been lying in wait for her. Putting on her best, unfazed smile, Heather went straight to her bedroom to change. Her mother didn't take the hint, maneuvering her wheelchair into the room directly behind her.

"She volunteered," Heather answered, deliberately not looking at her mother as she pulled one of her better, less-used dresses out of the closet. "Thought you might need it." Moving swiftly, something that having two children close together had taught her how to do, she took off her skirt and blouse and slipped on the navy-blue dress. "I thought it was nice of her."

"Nice," Martha snorted. "All the woman wanted to do was pump me for information."

Angling the zipper up, Heather paused only for a second to look at her mother. Had coming over here with the medication been a ruse to get answers to some questions Ursula had about her and Ben?

"What kind of information?" Heather asked, trying to sound nonchalant.

Martha frowned, once more following her, this time out of the room. "She asked how I was."

Heather silently released the breath she'd been holding. Everything was still all right. "That's not a crime, mother. That's being polite."

The look on Martha's face darkened. "That's being nosy."

Heather knew this line of conversation could drag on indefinitely. She didn't have the time to indulge her mother.

"Girls!" she called. "Come out here. I need to see you." She looked at her mother. "Then you didn't tell her how you were?"

Hannah and Hayley came running in from the backyard. Both looked reasonably clean. Nothing a little water and a hairbrush couldn't fix. She could feel her nerves channeling themselves into excitement.

"I told her that my daughter forgot to pick up my medication, but that didn't seem to faze that dreadful woman, seeing as how she brought it."

Her mother could take silk purses and turn them into sow's ears. Taking a paper towel, Heather wet it and then swiftly applied the dampened area to Hayley's slightly dirty cheeks. "Like I said, Ursula was being nice."

Unable to contain her curiosity any longer, Martha demanded, "What are you doing?"

"Getting ready," Heather replied cheerfully. "The

girls and I are going out." The moment her words were out, the two girls began to shift excitedly.

"Out? Out where?" Martha asked. Heather spent her evenings at home every night. A change in pattern tended to make her uneasy.

"To eat dinner at Lily's." She looked at her daughters, two bolts of lightning just dying to be released. "Would you like that, girls?"

In response, both girls clapped their hands together joyfully.

Martha's frown only deepened. "Lily's? You just came from there. You just spent all day *working* there," she reminded her.

Heather finished brushing Hayley's hair and turned her attention to Hannah. "I know."

Martha sighed dramatically. "Besides, I don't feel like going out."

Heather turned to look at her mother. "Then you're in luck, Mother," she replied sweetly. "Because you're not coming."

"You're not inviting me?"

"Sorry, I'm not the one doing the inviting." She set the brush down again. "And the one doing it invited just the girls and me."

"Who?" Martha asked as the girls cheered. "Who invited you out?"

Heather braced herself for the storm she knew was coming. "Ben Kerrigan."

Martha's mouth dropped. "That juvenile delinquent who answered the phone?"

"He's over thirty, Mother," Heather patiently pointed out.

Martha raised her chin haughtily. "Doesn't change what he was and probably still is."

Ordinarily, Heather would have kept her mouth shut. There was no winning an argument with her mother. But tonight was different. She'd had enough of the woman's high-handed ways. "Ben Kerrigan was never a juvenile delinquent. He was and *is* someone with a zest for life."

A snort met her words. "Is that what they're calling it these days?" Hands on her wheels, Martha was about to propel herself into the kitchen. It was time for her dinner. "Well, doesn't matter. You can't go."

Heather's reply stopped her in midroll. "Mother, in case you haven't noticed, I'm over eighteen. I really don't need your permission to do anything."

Turning the wheelchair around, Martha dramatically clutched at her heart. "I'm not feeling well."

She'd been through this routine far too often. Heather began to herd her daughters toward the door. "I'll be at Lily's. If there's a real emergency, you can reach me there. Or, better yet, why don't you call—"

Heather never finished her statement. There was a knock on the door. Flustered, she prayed it wasn't Ben. She wanted a few minutes away from her mother to center herself. To look like something a little better than a harried mother of two and a put-upon daughter.

Why the effort? It's not like this is going to go anywhere.

Thinking that it was Ben, as well, her mother ordered, "Tell him to go away."

"Mama?" Hannah said in an uncertain voice.

"We're going, girls," Heather responded, quieting their fears.

But when she opened the door, it wasn't Ben on the other side but Ursula. The moment the door opened, the woman breezed in.

"Hi, this is short notice, I know," she said quickly, nodding at the little girls and addressing her words to Heather, "but I was wondering if your mother was free this evening."

Mother is always free, especially with her criticism, Heather thought. She stepped back, allowing Ursula to see her mother.

"Oh, there you are, Martha," Ursula said, crossing over to her. "Yuri's cousin Jan is visiting from one of those provinces in Canada, I forget which one," she confided. "But we need a fourth."

"A fourth what?" Martha snapped.

"I'll explain everything as soon as they get here," Ursula promised. She looked at Heather. "Shouldn't you and the girls be going right about now?"

Stunned, Heather could only look at the postmistress. "How did you—"

Ursula's smile was nothing short of serene. "I'm

the postmistress, dear. By now you should know that nothing happens in this town without my knowing it."

"You're a busybody, that's what you are," Martha informed her haughtily.

"Mother!" Heather cried, embarrassed.

But Ursula seemed completely undaunted by the blunt accusation. "I prefer 'student of human nature' myself. Now, let's get you into something a little more stylish than that robe you're wearing," Ursula suggested. Not waiting for a comment and certainly not for any sign of agreement, she took hold of the back of Martha's wheelchair and began to push her out of the room. Ignoring the sputtered protests, she made her way toward the guest room and said to Heather. "Keep him waiting a little while, but not too long, dear," she advised. "Men like to anticipate but not stew."

Feeling a little like Cinderella being liberated by her fairy godmother, Heather took each daughter by the hand and made her getaway.

Chapter Seven

Hayley talked almost nonstop all the way to the restaurant. Occasionally, Hannah chimed in, as well. Going out was a big deal for her children, and Heather had a feeling that getting them to bed tonight was going to be a huge challenge. But it did her heart good to see them this excited.

It also helped her forget that she was nervous.

As they walked into Lily's, Hayley's steady stream of chatter abruptly halted.

"Are we getting a shot?" Hayley asked, suspicion coloring her small features the moment Ben joined them.

He laughed as he ruffled Hayley's hair. "Not unless you want one."

Hayley shook her head so hard, her silky, strawberry-blond hair fairly flew back and forth about her small face. "No!"

"How about you, Hannah?" Ben asked, looking at her sister. "Would you like one?"

Hannah's deep-green eyes widened to the size of the proverbial saucers. She took a step closer to her mother, but this time, didn't hide behind her. "No, thank you."

Ben didn't know which little girl amused him more. He looked at Heather. "Polite, even in her uncertainty. Reminds me of you."

Heather wished she could believe she had left an impression on him, but he was just being charming, nothing more. She summoned a glib smile, the same one she used when the miners would flirt with her when she waited on them.

"You never knew me well enough to have anything remind you of me," Heather pointed out.

Ben opened the door for her and her daughters, standing back until they had all filed by. His eyes washed over her as she passed. "You'd be surprised."

The moment they entered, the din surrounded them, but she still heard him. Still picked out the sound of his voice. His answer seemed to ripple along her skin, causing the tiny hairs on her arms and the back of her neck to stand up at attention. As if in anticipation.

Down girl, she ordered herself. He didn't mean anything by that. He was just being Ben, nothing more. Charming and seductive as ever. She sincerely doubted that he even remembered they had made love that one night. But her reason refused to prevail. Her nerves continued to jump around.

A fine way for the mother of two to react, she upbraided herself.

"There, that table," Hayley declared, her daughter's enthusiasm slicing through the serious mood building within her.

The little girl pointed her finger at a table where they usually sat whenever they came to the restaurant. Ordinarily, Lily's was not filled to capacity. This time a couple sat at "their" table.

Heather vaguely recognized the young couple as people who had been several grades ahead of her in high school. Hades was a very small town where almost every face was familiar if not well-known. She glanced around. There were no other available tables. Lily was probably being run ragged. She should be here, pitching in, not acting like a customer, Heather thought.

Very gently she pushed Hayley's hand down. She'd told the girl countless times not to point. "Honey, there's someone sitting at the table. We'll get the next one that's free."

"But I want that one," Hayley said, pouting. "It's our special table," she insisted. Hayley cocked her head as she looked up at her mother. "You said so."

"We can't always have what we want," Heather told her younger daughter patiently.

She silently prayed that Hayley wasn't going to start carrying on and causing a scene. Under normal circumstances, it wouldn't embarrass her. There wasn't a parent alive who hadn't endured at least one tantrum at the hands of their child. But she hated the thought of it happening in front of Ben. She wanted him to like her children, to see them as little people, not nuisances.

Why? What difference can it possibly make? Having no answer that was acceptable, Heather locked away the taunting voice.

"Amen to that," Ben said.

Heather looked at him sharply, wondering if she'd just imagined him saying that. The next moment he was kneeling down to Hayley's level.

"Do you really want that table, Hayley?"

The little girl bobbed her head up and down. With the sixth sense of a child who knew she was going to get her way, her eyes never left the face of her new knight in shining armor.

Ben rose to his feet again. Heather looked at him uneasily. "Ben, what are you going to do? She has to learn to be patient. We can't just—"

The rest of her protest dried up as Ben flashed her that grin that went straight to the center of her stomach.

"Maybe we can," he told her. "Just this once. Stay here."

Stunned and speechless, she watched Ben walk over to the table that Hayley considered her personal property. Everything about his body language was engaging as he spoke with Bill and Susan Jessop, the people who were seated at Hayley's table. Before she could wonder if Ben remembered them, she saw the hearty exchange of greetings, followed by a very short, friendly conversation. And then the couple rose, vacating the table.

Hayley was jumping up and down beside her, clapping her hands together. "He did it! He did it!"

The next moment Ben beckoned her and the girls to join him. Hayley flew over on feet that barely seemed to touch the floor.

"Ben, what did you say to them?" Heather asked as she and Hannah caught up.

The adulation that shone in Hayley's eyes warmed his heart in a way that caught him by surprise. "That this was my first night back and that I was celebrating with an old friend and her daughters, one of whom had her heart set on sitting at her 'special' table. I told them I'd pick up the tab for their meal if I could have this table. They were finished anyway and thought it was a good deal."

But she wasn't an old friend, at least, not in his eyes. Why would he go to all this trouble for her daughter. "Why?" she said out loud.

"Because I could never resist the soulful look of a lovely lady," Ben answered.

After taking Hayley's small hand, he brought it to

his lips and kissed it lightly, continental style. Hayley looked utterly entranced, holding her hand with her other one as if the limb had suddenly turned to gold. Not to leave Hannah out, Ben kissed her hand, as well.

It was the first time both her daughters had been rendered speechless at the same time. The man was a miracle worker, Heather thought.

"You have two very lovely daughters, Heather," he told her.

She doubted if he had any idea how much his words pleased her. But she had to be practical. She was going to be their mother long after this Prince Charming disappeared into the night, leaving her to deal with the aftermath of his actions.

"Yes, thank you, I know that and I don't want to see them become spoiled."

His smile was warm, intimate, somehow causing the eighty or so patrons in the restaurant to vanish into nothingness as if they'd never existed.

"One time isn't going to spoil them," he assured her. "Takes a whole lot more than that, trust me."

Trust me. Now there was an ironic line, coming from a man who'd made her world stand still, only to disappear from it almost the next instant.

She looked at Hayley, then glanced over toward Hannah as both girls scrambled up, taking opposite sides of the booth. Both girls resembled love-struck puppies, gazing at Ben as if he were the reigning teen idol.

In a way he was. For as long as she could remember, Ben had always been every woman's fantasy in Hades. And he'd just gotten himself a new generation of fans.

"You girls aren't spoiled, are you?" Ben asked, glancing from one to the other, his expression dead serious. The girls vigorously shook their heads in unison. He grinned and looked at Heather. "I rest my case."

Ben hadn't lost his touch. If anything, he had perfected the ability to seduce a woman with a single word, a single look. Echoes of the one night that they had spent together came back to her. It was a night she relived in her mind time and again, despite all her efforts to leave it in the past.

But the memories refused to stay buried. Instead they were always in front of her. Every time she looked at Hannah, she could see traces of Ben in her face. Was reminded of the night the child had come into existence.

"Heather, so you did come back. And you brought the girls."

Turning, Heather saw that Lily had come up behind them and was now smiling a greeting at her daughters. The woman looked a great deal better than she had this morning.

"We got our special table, Aunt Lily," Hayley told her, scrambling up on her knees.

Not to be left out, Hannah added, "Dr. Ben got it for us."

Lily looked amused. "Looks like 'Dr. Ben' has a lot of magic tricks up his sleeve."

Hayley's jaw dropped low enough to almost touch the table. The look in her eyes was pure hero worship. "You do magic, too?"

"Sometimes." He winked at both girls. And then he looked up at the petite woman standing beside their table. The chalky pallor was gone from her face. "You look a lot better this evening, Lily."

"Thanks to you," she acknowledged. "Ginger really works."

Ben picked up a menu and opened it. "Glad I could help."

"Dinner is on the house," Lily told them, wanting to show her appreciation.

Hannah frowned at her mother's friend. Unlike Hayley, she was not one to buck authority. "We have to sit on the roof?"

Heather bit back a laugh. "No, honey, that's just an expression Aunt Lily used. It means we don't have to pay for dinner."

"You paying for dinner was never part of the plan," Ben informed her. "This was going to be my treat. I never ask a lady out if I don't intend to pay."

"Well, tonight your money's no good here," Lily told him. "I haven't felt this good in four months." She looked at Heather's daughters. "Order anything you like." Just before Lily stepped away, she leaned over and whispered to Heather, "Good luck."

Wanting to protest the assumption she knew Lily

had just made, she succeeded only in getting the air caught in her throat.

Ben lowered his menu, raising his eyes to Heather. "What did she say?"

Heather pressed her lips together, deliberately avoiding making eye contact. "Nothing."

"Couldn't be nothing," he said easily. "You're turning crimson."

"No, she's not," Hannah contradicted after eyeing her mother. "Mama's turning red."

Amused, Ben took it upon himself to broaden the little girl's world a shade. He put it in terms he thought she would relate to. "Crimson's in the red family. It's a deep, dark red."

The look on Hayley's face told Heather that her daughter was taking in Ben's words as if he were Moses on the Mount, coming down with a second set of commandments. Observing, Heather could only shake her head as she laughed shortly to herself. No female was immune to Ben.

Catching the expression on her face, his eyes narrowed. "What?"

Heather gestured to his small audience of two. "You have them eating out of your hand."

"No, we're not, Mama," Hannah protested, bewildered. "We're eating out of the dish." She pointed to the plate that held the hot dinner rolls that Lily had served with every meal. The girls had each already claimed one and were busy making them disappear, bit by bit.

Heather pretended to take the correction in stride. "My mistake."

Her eyes met Ben's. The amusement she saw there took her completely prisoner. She should have realized that he could very easily storm her ramparts with just a look. Just as he had seven years ago. Seeing him being so nice to her girls made her feel she was in jeopardy of losing her heart to him all over again.

As if her heart had ever truly been hers after that night by the lake. Even all those years while she lay in Joe's bed, trying to be the wife the miner both needed and deserved, a piece of her had always belonged to Ben. Would have belonged to him, she knew, even if they'd never shared that night together.

At the ripe old age of fourteen and a half, around the same time that her father had finally left her mother, she'd fallen for Ben. From that time forward, there had been no turning back for her, no recapturing what had been lost. She could only try to make the best of it.

And the best was definitely here tonight. Heather listened to her girls, even Hannah, talk up a storm as they competed for Ben's attention.

A little more than two hours later, as Ben brought them home, Heather realized this night would be one she would press between the pages of her memory, to take out and examine whenever her heart needed lifting.

Unbeknownst to Ben, she'd sat back at Lily's and watched him interact with her girls, pretending that he was not only Hannah's father but Hayley's, as well. Pretending, too, that she belonged to him not just in spirit, but by lawful decree.

She had allowed her heart to embrace the thought that they were actually a family unit. It had been a lovely fantasy. But now the evening was over and she had to box up her fantasies and place them out of reach.

She turned in her seat and looked behind her. Secure in their car seats, Hannah and Hayley had both fallen asleep. "I never thought it would happen. They're both worn-out at the same time."

Ben pulled her car up into her driveway. Despite her protests, he'd insisted on driving them home, saying it was a nice night and that he would walk back to his brother's home. It was only a mile, and daylight was only now slipping away.

She undid her seat belt, fumbling for a second because she was used to finding the release on her right, not the left. "It'll just take me a minute to carry Hannah in. I'll be right back for Hayley."

But he had no intention of letting her carry in both girls while he sat back. He was out of the car, rounding the hood and opening her door before she had a chance to do it herself.

"I'll carry them in," he told her. His tone said that he wasn't about to debate the offer. He undid the belts that secured Hannah in her seat, then lifted her out, careful not to wake the little girl. "To tell you the truth, I was beginning to have my doubts that they were capable of being tired out."

"Same thought crosses my mind," Heather confessed. "A lot."

After lifting Hayley out of her seat, Heather made her way to the front door behind Ben. Under the guise of pretending to search for her keys, Heather covertly took in the sight of Ben holding Hannah in his arms. Her heart swelled.

If only…

With lightning speed, she banked down the thought. She couldn't allow herself to go there. There was no "if only." Everyone believed that Hannah had been Joe's daughter. *Hannah* believed she was Joe's daughter. She had to leave it at that.

"What are you doing?" Ben asked.

"Looking for my keys." In earnest this time, she stretched her fingers down to the bottom of her purse.

"I've got them," he reminded her, holding the key ring out to her. "I drove, remember?"

She flushed but said nothing as she took the keys from him. Opening the door, she motioned for him to follow her. "Their room's this way," she told him in a whisper.

Walking through the living room to the staircase, Heather half expected to be waylaid by her mother. But there was no sign of Martha Ryan, no sound of the wheelchair crossing the wooden floor. Heather released the breath she'd been holding as she went up to the room that her girls shared. The inquisition had been placed on hold. Temporarily.

Once she gently deposited Hayley in her junior bed, she slipped off the girl's shoes and then simply covered her with the comforter. Finished, she moved over to Hannah's bed, only to see that Ben had already taken off the little girl's shoes and was covering her just as she'd done with Hayley. She smiled, nodding her approval.

Ben lowered his head in order to reach her ear. "Think they'll sleep until morning?"

A shiver slithered through her, but she managed not to react. "God willing," she murmured, turning on the fairy-princess lamp that stood between the two beds. Both girls were afraid of the dark. The lamp was the compromise that they had struck.

Turning from the beds, Ben placed his hand on the small of her back and guided her out.

Every single pulse point and nerve ending in her body focused itself on that part of her anatomy. She reminded herself to breathe.

Heather softly closed the door once they were outside the room. "Most mothers would have gotten them into their pajamas," Ben commented.

She'd learned long ago that some rules could be bent in order to achieve the desired end result.

"Most mothers don't have junior commandos who run on ever-recharging batteries for children." This was not the first time her girls had slept in their clothes. "Clothes can be washed, wrinkles can be ironed out."

He laughed. "Practical as well as beautiful."

"Stop."

"Stop what?" Without thinking, he pushed back the curl that fell into her face.

She willed her knees to return to their previous solid state and concentrated on the words and not the butterflies.

"That," she said thickly. "You don't have to say nice things to me."

"Somehow, putting a curse on you and your entire lineage didn't seem the way to go after the evening we shared tonight." His eyes on hers, Ben's smile softened, growing intimate. Heather felt her heart leap high into her throat. "Why wouldn't I want to say nice things to you?"

Words floated away from her brain like so many shards of ice, melting into nothingness. She shrugged. "You don't have to."

"Why don't you leave that decision to me?" he suggested.

Before she could answer, before she could even draw a single breath into her suddenly oxygen-depleted lungs, Ben was framing her face with his hands, mingling her space with his own.

And then, just like that, there was no space left between them at all.

Chapter Eight

The moment Ben's lips touched hers, Heather felt transported back to that magical evening they had shared. Closing her eyes, she could see the whole scene unfolding: the golden rays of the sun had begun to lengthen across the lake like long, thin fingers.

It had been warm then, too. So warm she felt as if her very skin would melt. And her heart had pounded exactly this way, desperate for air that was nowhere to be had.

Allowing herself to remember, to savor, to relive, Heather stood on tiptoe, lacing her arms around Ben's neck.

Lacing her heart to the moment.

She could feel the heat radiating from his body, growing in intensity. Felt, too, the long-dormant desires springing up like fresh buds through the newly tilled, newly nurtured earth.

She was his for the taking. Just as she had been years ago. But this was wrong and she couldn't allow herself to get swept away. And she wouldn't, Heather resolved. She'd stay right here with her feet firmly planted on the ground, the mother of two, a level-headed, responsible adult—in a minute from now.

Just one sweet, sugar-coated minute. That was all she wanted.

She wasn't asking so much, was she? To feel desirable, to feel beautiful. To *feel*. Just for the briefest time. Heather surrendered herself to the moment, swearing she could find her way back.

Ben had lost count of the number of women he'd kissed throughout his life. Not that they had all blended together into some huge, swirling cauldron in his mind. In one fashion or another, he'd cared about all the women who had passed through his life. He enjoyed kissing women, enjoyed making love with them when the occasion arose.

He loved women, period. And they had always, always returned the compliment.

Despite the number, there were things, however minute, that set them apart from one another. And he could distinctly remember making love with Heather. Distinctly remember the flavor of her lips, the sweetness that poured through his veins when he'd held her, when he'd kissed her. Remember the fire that arose when he explored the secrets of her body. Both his own fire and hers. That night she had been an arousing combination of innocence and eagerness. It had excited him beyond description.

He was excited to rediscover her sweetness. He could taste it in her kiss. She was still innocent. And still eager.

But now she had an extra layer. Just beyond the perimeter, Ben detected a wariness. Not quite distrust, not quite trust.

Life had done that to her, Ben thought.

Life had left a mark on all of them.

Though he knew everyone perceived him to be the very personification of confidence, his experience with Lila had left a deep, grave mark on him.

Lila had been the first woman he had ever loved to the point that he wanted to settle down, to devote himself only to her. When she'd refused to marry him, only live together, he'd accepted it. Because he'd loved her. And she had taken that love and thrown it back in his face when she'd taken off. Deserted him not once but twice.

The first time had been when she'd left Hades. He'd pulled himself together and pretended so hard that it didn't matter that eventually, he'd come to believe his nonchalance. Until she returned. The second time she'd left him, he had been completely devastated, although he never admitted it to anyone, not even to himself. At least, not to the full extent of his wounds. He'd declared Lila legally dead in his mind. Although he didn't think himself capable of giving his heart again, he sure relished this moment with Heather.

The kiss deepened, moving from friendly contact to something more. Ben's breath grew short and his blood heated. He caught himself wishing that they could be back at the lake again.

But they weren't. They were on the doorstep of the house that her late husband had built for her. With the two little girls she and Joe had created sleeping a few yards away.

He couldn't allow this to go further, no matter how much he wanted it to.

Still holding her to him, Ben drew his lips from hers. The sensation of loss whispered over him. He smiled into her eyes, seeing himself mirrored there. "You still pack quite a punch, Heather."

Her insides were shaking. Heather drew in a long breath. Her eyes fluttered closed for a second as she sealed his touch within her soul.

Resistance is futile. The mantra echoed through her brain. She did her best to ignore it.

"So do you," she replied.

The old Heather would never have been able to find her tongue, much less say anything as glib as that. But the old Heather had wanted nothing more that to bask in the light of his smile. There had been no responsibilities, no thought given to consequences.

Her mouth curved as the irony mocked her. She'd been a babe in the woods. The consequences of her actions had been a baby. The greatest gift she could have ever received.

The yearning inside reminded her that she was still a young woman. A woman with needs that had suddenly exploded into existence. She struggled to overcome them as best as she could. It wasn't easy. Not when he was looking at her like that. Smiling at her like that.

Ben loosened his hold on her waist. "I'd better let you go in before I give in to the temptation to carry you off to the lake."

Her eyes widened. "You remember that?"

"Of course I remember that." Reluctant to break contact completely, his hands rested on the soft swell of her hips. Two children and she felt as small, as delicate as she had that night. "You left a very big impression on me, Heather."

He could lie so smoothly, Heather thought. And she would have given anything to believe him. But she knew better. All she had been was a momentary diversion in his life.

"So big that you ran off with Lila less than a month later."

The moment the words were out of her mouth, she regretted them. Regretted them because they reopened his wound and made her seem petty. She wasn't petty. All she had ever wanted was for him to be happy.

"I'm sorry, I had no business saying that." She offered a fleeting, tight smile. "It's just that I know my place in the scheme of things."

Ben had been her first lover. Her only lover, except for Joe and he had come afterward. She had no vast experience to dazzle him with, no beauty to take his breath away. A man could hardly be expected to remember someone like that.

Ben paused, studying the face of the woman before him. She was so devoid of conceit, she took his breath away. He hadn't returned to Hades to pick up any threads, to relive any past liaisons. He'd returned to make amends with Shayne and to try to find himself, to find the person he'd once been and perhaps even the one he was meant to be.

But none of that had anything to do with resuming a relationship. And then he'd seen Heather.

Her choice of words intrigued him. "Your 'place' in the scheme of things?" he repeated, mystified. "There's no caste system in Hades, Heather. Frozen or not, this is still the United States. Places here are interchangeable." He grinned. "It's guaranteed under the constitution, or the Declaration of Independence, or maybe by the Cookie Monster, I don't know. All I know is that life is fluid and there is no such thing as—" The stark, bright beams from the headlights of an approaching car interrupted his train of thought.

Noticing the disappointment that burrowed deeply in her chest, Heather turned to see who was coming over at this hour.

Shading her eyes, she recognized the SUV as being the same one that had been parked in her driveway several hours earlier when she and the girls had made their escape, avoiding any more of her mother's recriminations.

What was Ursula doing back here again?

Curious, Heather came down the three steps and approached the vehicle just as Ursula got out of the rear passenger seat.

"Is there anything wrong, Ursula?"

The door on the other side opened at the same time. A tall, stately looking man with a full head of white hair, very lively blue eyes and an infectious smile got out. Except for the white hair, he appeared almost boyish. Even with the vehicle separating them, it was easy to see that he towered over Ursula. The stranger hurried around the rear of the vehicle, shouting something to the driver in a language Heather couldn't make out. The next moment the rear door popped open.

As Heather watched, the stranger took a wheelchair out, lifting it as if it weighed nothing. At the same time, Ursula was opening the front passenger door.

"That's my mother's wheelchair," Heather said to Ben. Her eyes widened further as she saw the passenger in the front seat. "And that's my mother."

Heather's mouth dropped open. Was she dreaming? Had all of this, the evening, the kiss and now seeing her mother somewhere other than in the house, all been just a dream? "Mother?"

Struggling not to look as if she was holding on to Ursula's strong forearms, Martha grumbled as she unsteadily gained her feet for the transfer from car to wheelchair. Her angry glare swept over Ursula and her daughter alike. "Damn woman and her friends kidnapped me."

By now the man had set her wheelchair on the ground and rolled it over to her side of the vehicle. With a polite smile, he edged Ursula out of the way then easily guided Martha into the chair.

"Doing fine, Mar-ta." The heavily accented, encouraging words were uttered much like a rallying cheer at a baseball game.

Ursula beamed in Heather's direction, patting the young woman's hand. There was a very pleased note in her voice as she assured Heather, "She had a wonderful time."

Martha was quick to contradict the statement. "I'm going to press charges."

Ben grinned, easily placing his hands on Heather's shoulders as he stood directly behind her. "Might not be all that easy to do," he warned Martha. "Don't forget, Max is her grandson."

Confused by her mother's sudden, unexpected appearance, Heather still couldn't help reacting to the fact that Ben was behaving as if they were a couple. She struggled to hold on to the moment. Did friends kiss friends the way he had kissed her?

Martha glared at the postmistress. "You had no business taking me out."

Ursula was cheerful, waving a hand at the accusation. "Nonsense, everyone needs to get out. To have a little fun. You're not dead yet, Martha. No reason to fold your hands on your chest and act as if you were." Shifting, Ursula raised her eyes away from the woman in the wheelchair to Heather. "No reason at all," she emphasized softly.

Tiny nerves danced through Heather. No, she was far from dead. Very far from dead. Her reaction to Ben's kiss had just proven that. She prayed that the darkening skies would hide the color she felt creeping into her face again.

She did her best to divert attention from herself. "Where did you take her?"

"They took me to that filthy saloon that no-account runs," Martha grumbled.

"He's not a 'no-account.' Ike owns several businesses in Hades along with his cousin, Mother." Embarrassment fluttered through her.

"Doesn't change what he is," Martha snorted.

"Your mother holds her drinks like a farm girl." The testimony, delivered with admiration, came from the tall stranger who still had a hand on her mother's wheelchair. It was obvious by his tone that he held farm girls in very high regard.

The next moment, a shy smile curved the

generous mouth beneath the white mustache. "I am sorry. Where are my manners? I am Janek, Yuri's…" He paused a moment, searching for the word that eluded him. And then he beamed. "Cousine."

"Cousin," Ursula corrected with a smile. Looking at Heather, she explained, although by no means with any sort of apologetic note, "English isn't Jan's first language."

Martha snorted disparagingly. "It's not exactly his second, either." Her expression remained sour as she wrapped her arms around herself.

"Jan speaks five languages," Ursula informed Ben and Heather proudly. "Just like my Yuri." She glanced over toward the man who was sitting behind the wheel of the vehicle they had just vacated. In response, Yuri waved at them. He appeared perfectly content to remain where he was until Ursula was ready to leave.

The windows were partially down. Enough for Heather to see the adoring look on the old miner's face. It occurred to her that the couple, well into their seventh decade, were acting like a pair of teenagers warmly wrapped in their first crush.

She envied them.

"Well, what are you waiting for?" Martha demanded hotly. "Winter?" She twisted around in her seat, looking over her shoulder at Jan. She gestured toward the ramp that her late son-in-law had built for her. "Push my wheelchair up the ramp." It was an order, not a request.

Heather winced. She wouldn't have blamed Yuri's cousin for leaving her mother right where she was and walking away.

"I have better idea. Ursula, would you please to hold the chair?" Jan asked.

"Hold the chair?" Martha repeated. "Why should she hold the chair? I said push, not stand still. Can't you hear, either?"

"I hear," Jan told her. "I hear very good." But instead of doing what she'd demanded, Jan leaned over and picked Martha up in his arms.

Panic stamped its mark on her mother's face and in her voice. Unsteady without the chair beneath her, she clutched Jan's neck. "What are you doing?"

"Taking you up the stairs the way a lady should be taken," Jan replied simply, as Ursula drew the wheelchair back out of his way.

About to voice her own protest, Heather felt Ben give her shoulder a light squeeze, as if to tell her to hold off for a moment. She didn't know which action surprised her more, Ben's or Jan's.

"You're too old," Martha protested, holding on to his neck for dear life. "Put me back! You'll get a heart attack."

"You are light, like feather," Jan told her. "My heart will not be attacking." He came to a stop before the front door. Behind him, Ursula had brought the wheelchair up the ramp and locked it into position. Jan easily deposited the woman in his arms onto the chair, then unlocked the wheels. "And I am not so old as you think, Mar-ta," he added, bringing his face down close to hers, his eyes twinkling.

It was the first time Heather had ever seen her mother at a loss for words. And the first time she had seen her mother blush. But there it was, illuminated by the front porch light. A pink hue claimed both cheeks. Heather turned her face toward Ursula, lowering her voice so that her mother couldn't hear. "You're a miracle worker, Ursula."

The postmistress shrugged. "Like I told your mother, I'm just a student of human nature, Heather." Her smile widened, and she turned her attention to Ben. "Now, boy, are you going to need a ride to your brother's house or are you planning on spending the night here with Heather?"

He pretended not to see the nervous, dismayed look on Heather's face. "I'd appreciate a ride back if it's not taking you out of your way."

"Not a problem, Doc. Hop in. There's plenty of room in the back."

Walking down the steps, she crossed to the vehicle, beckoning Jan to follow. He said something in his native tongue to Martha, then hurried down the steps. Leaving Martha looking bewildered and frustrated.

Ursula made the necessary introduction. "Jan, Yuri, this is Doc Shayne's younger brother. Doc Ben. He's going to be staying around for a while, right, Doc?" She turned her face up to Ben.

He merely laughed. "You know everything better than I do, Ursula."

"Comes from paying close attention," the woman informed him with a hearty chuckle. She glanced over her shoulder just before slipping into the car and assuming the shotgun position. "See you soon, Martha."

To Heather's surprise, no sarcastic or bitter remark met the other woman's words. Her mother merely snorted and pivoted her wheelchair around so that it faced the front door.

"Well, open it," she snapped at Heather, who obliged.

"Your mother, she is a lovely woman," Jan called out to her.

Depends on your definition of *lovely,* Heather thought. She turned and waved at the occupants of the departing car before following her mother inside. Jan returned the wave. With a fleeting note of disappointment, she saw Ben was already in the car.

As she followed her mother inside and locked the door behind them, Heather couldn't help wondering what Ike was putting into his drinks these days. "Lovely woman" indeed.

"Did you have a nice time, Mother?" Heather heard herself ask. When there was no immediate answer, she decided her mother must still be in the throes of her out-of-body experience, brought about by equal parts shock and amusement. Even before her mother's disease had laid waste to her body, Martha Ryan had never gone out, never mingled with the other people of Hades. She had spent all her free time staring at the walls of bitterness and self-pity, lashing out at anyone who crossed her path.

Ursula, Yuri and this Jan person had to be the bravest people she'd ever met, Heather thought.

"Nice time?" Martha echoed, swinging her wheelchair around to face her. "What kind of question is that? The stupid fool can't even say my name right. 'Mar-ta,'" she mimicked the sound of Jan's voice. "Sounds like a damn speech impediment."

Heather noticed that her mother didn't actually come out and answer her question. Instead she'd created a diversion. Had the woman actually enjoyed herself? Oh God, she hoped so.

"I read somewhere that Russians and people born in Poland have trouble pronouncing 'th' because the letters don't appear together in their languages."

Martha's scowl intensified. "Anyone with an ear can hear he has trouble with it."

For once Heather decided not to back down or drop the subject. She was tired of avoidance being the rule of thumb around her mother.

"So, beyond the fact that Yuri's cousin mangled your name, did you have a nice time?"

"What kind of question is that?"

"A very legitimate one, Mother." She felt the way the girls had earlier this evening, when they'd clapped their hands and jumped up and down. This restored her faith in miracles. "Did you have a nice time?" she repeated, saying each word slowly.

An Important Message from the Editors

Dear Reader,

Because you've chosen to read one of our fine romance novels, we'd like to say "thank you!" And, as a **special** way to thank you, we've selected <u>two more</u> of the books you love so well **plus** two exciting Mystery Gifts to send you— absolutely <u>FREE!</u>

Please enjoy them with our compliments...

Pam Powers

Lift here

Peel off seal and place inside...

How to validate your Editor's "Thank You" FREE GIFTS

1. Peel off gift seal from front cover. Place it in space provided at right. This automatically entitles you to receive 2 FREE BOOKS and 2 FREE mystery gifts.

2. Send back this card and you'll get 2 new Silhouette *Special Edition®* novels. These books have a cover price of $4.99 or more each in the U.S. and $5.99 or more each in Canada, but they are yours to keep absolutely free.

3. There's no catch. You're under no obligation to buy anything. We charge nothing—ZERO—for your first shipment. And you don't have to make any minimum number of purchases—not even one!

4. The fact is, thousands of readers enjoy receiving their books by mail from The Silhouette Reader Service™. They enjoy the convenience of home delivery...they like getting the best new novels at discount prices BEFORE they're available in stores... and they love their Reader to Reader subscriber newsletter featuring author news, special book offers, book reviews and much more!

5. We hope that after receiving your free books you'll want to remain a subscriber. But the choice is yours— to continue or cancel, any time at all! So why not take us up on our invitation, with no risk of any kind. You'll be glad you did!

GET TWO *Free* MYSTERY GIFTS...

SURPRISE MYSTERY GIFTS COULD BE YOURS **FREE** AS A SPECIAL "THANK YOU" FROM THE EDITORS

"I survived," Martha snapped. "Just barely." Her eyes narrowed. "Now, don't bother me with silly questions. I'm tired. It's hours past my bedtime." She maneuvered her wheelchair around Heather and began to make her way toward the back of the house and her room. "Stupid woman. What gives her the right to think she could just barge in here and kidnap me out of my own home like that? I should press charges against her, grandson or no grandson. And if he won't listen to me, I can always call the sheriff's office in Anchorage. I'll show her she can't take advantage of a poor, defenseless woman like that." Martha's voice continued to echo down the hall as she headed to her room.

"You are many things, Mother," Heather said to herself, a smile playing on her lips as she crossed to the staircase, "but no one will ever accuse you of being defenseless. Not with that mouth."

Heather slowly made her way up the stairs. Her mother was right, it was time for bed and she might as well go, too. She doubted very much, however, that she would get any sleep tonight.

Not when her body was tingling this way.

Chapter Nine

Klondyke LeBlanc, known to one and all as Ike, tended to fill a room with his presence the moment he entered it. The crowded reception area of the medical clinic was no exception. Crossing to the nurse's desk, a short nine feet from the door, he fielded and returned more than a dozen greetings.

After nodding to Alison, he looked past her shoulder, scanning the corridor that ran parallel to her desk and fed into three of the examining rooms.

"Business or pleasure?" Alison asked.

Ike winked at her. "Pleasure, darlin', always pleasure."

Spotting the reason for his impromptu appearance at the clinic, Ike didn't stand on ceremony. Instead he went around Alison's desk and down the corridor.

Holding on to his glib tongue, he placed himself directly in Ben's path and waited until the younger man barely missed walking into him. Ike laughed heartily at the look of surprise on Ben's face. Demonstrative by nature, Ike grasped his hand and gave him a friendly pounding on the back.

"Ben Kerrigan, as I live and breathe." After releasing his hand, Ike took only half a step back. His keen eyes missed nothing as they swept over his best friend's younger brother. He'd done some growing, Ike thought. More than just a little. "Had to see it for myself. You're really back."

"Looks that way."

Ben laughed shortly. He'd always liked his brother's best friend. Always envied Shayne the bond the two had, despite the fact that Shayne was so close-mouthed, and Ike so outgoing.

Ike shook his head. "Hell, I'd have bet that a meteor would have hit the town square before you'd come back to Hades."

Ben's patient walked out, a somewhat smitten look on her face. Since he'd returned, Alison said that the patient load had almost doubled. The women of Hades were coming in with all sorts of minor complaints, real and imagined. Shayne commented that it was a waste of their professional time to see "non-patients" who were only there for a view of Ben.

With a cordial nod toward the young woman, Ben returned his attention to Ike. "I'm afraid you would have lost that bet."

"Obviously." Ike grinned. "So, you staying?"

Ben laughed shortly, but for once there was no humor in his eyes even though his mouth curved. "That depends on Shayne."

"Shayne?" Ike hadn't expected that to be a factor. "He's glad to have you back."

Because this was Ike, someone he'd known and in a way looked up to ever since he was a boy, Ben allowed his guard to slip just a little. "Certainly doesn't act that way."

Ike waved away the underlying notion. No way would Shayne have wanted his brother anywhere but here. The man was as family oriented as they came, always had been. "You know Shayne. Hard as nails on the outside—"

"Hard as nails on the inside," Shayne concluded, interrupting as he joined them. Picking up a folder, he held it out to Ben. "Room one's empty. You can see your next patient there. Unless, of course, you'd like to take off."

"Room one," Ben repeated stoically, taking the chart from his brother.

Ike shook his head. "He's trying, Shayne. Cut him some slack."

Shayne looked at his best friend sharply. He resented the advice. Ordinarily Ike didn't dispense any unless asked. This wasn't the time for the man to start changing his habits.

"I've been cutting him slack all his life, Ike, and all he's ever done was trip me up with it. Now, if you have some kind of a complaint, I can try to fit you in," Shayne offered. "Otherwise, you're taking up space and you're in the way."

They'd been friends far too long for Ike to take offense. This was only Shayne's facade. Ike glanced at Ben.

"I can see why you came back. You missed your brother's winning personality." He saw Shayne open his mouth again and got to the reason for his visit before he was asked to leave again. "I'm just here to invite you to the Salty Dog tonight. You remember the rules, Ben. You're not officially back until we have a party in your honor. Seeing as how you've been here, what?" Life in Hades went by a different clock, a different calendar. Time varied between standing still and racing, although it was usually the former. "Almost three weeks—"

"A month," Ben corrected. "It's been almost a month." He'd even gotten his own place, even though Sydney and the kids had urged him to remain with them as long as he wanted. He was hoping things between Shayne and him would go better if they weren't together 24/7.

Ike laughed to himself. "Probably seems a lot longer than that with Shayne riding you." He saw the warning look come into Shayne's eyes. "Okay, tonight." He stepped into the waiting room. "You're all invited," he announced to anyone within hearing range.

As it was with all of the parties thrown at Ike and Luc's establishment, the whole town was invited. And for the most part, a good portion of the five hundred plus residents turned out for at least a part of the evening. While mining was still Hades's main industry, socializing was the main source of entertainment, the movie theater notwithstanding.

"That includes you, too, Shayne." Ike's hand was still on the doorknob as he eyed his friend pointedly. "Marta will take it as nothing short of an insult if you don't show up."

Shayne snorted, picking up a folder of his own. "Marta won't even notice if I'm not there. She's too busy watching you flirt with every female who passes through the Salty's double doors."

Ike's grin grew wider. His life had taken on a great deal more color since the diminutive school-teacher had come into it.

"She knows it's all just part of the charm of the place—and me." Crossing back to the reception desk, he lowered his voice a little. "And she also knows that it's harmless. Lord knows, Marta's more than enough woman for me and you can tell Sydney I said so, seeing as how they're still best friends."

It was because of Sydney that Marta had come to Hades in the first place. For a short stay initially. It had turned into the stay without end rather quickly and nobody was happier about that than he was.

"After Sydney introduced her to you, I don't understand how that's still possible," Shayne commented.

Ike opened the front door. "Be there," he ordered before letting himself out.

"We'll see." It was as much of a promise as Shayne was willing to make at the moment. Watching his brother work a room would take a certain mind set on his part now. Gone were the days when he was proud of the way every eye turned to look at Ben in unabashed admiration.

As if coming to, Ben looked at the name on top of his folder. Another woman, he thought. He certainly hoped this wasn't another nonexistent malady used as a flimsy excuse to get close.

"June," Ben read the name jotted across the fairly thin folder.

In response, not one but two figures rose from their places in the waiting room, June Yearling Quintano and her husband, Kevin. He tried to take his wife's elbow to assist her since she was rather heavy at this point in her pregnancy and the chair she'd been sitting on didn't have arms for her to grip.

With a tight smile, June drew her elbow away. She was stubborn and took a great deal of pride in being independent. She dug herself out of the chair and walked into the inner office ahead of Kevin.

She had on a pair of denim overalls. The same kind of overalls, albeit a couple of annoying sizes larger now, that she'd worn while running her original auto-repair shop. She'd sold the place just before she'd met Kevin, who was the owner of Hades's only airline service. But people still came to her, complaining that the person she'd sold her shop to wasn't nearly as good as she was. Finding herself fixing vehicles for free, June decided that maybe making a go of the old family farm wasn't her true destiny after all.

Shortly before she discovered she was pregnant, she bought back her shop. Despite her condition, she was at the shop every day.

"She was supposed to be only supervising at this point," Kevin told Ben once they were inside the exam room and June had gotten onto the table to have her vital signs taken and recorded. "That was the agreement. She's not supposed to be lying on a dolly, sliding under a car to fix whatever's wrong with its undercarriage," Kevin complained.

"I only did it once," June said defensively. "Two months ago."

Kevin threw up his hands. He'd gotten married later than most, having first raised his sisters and brother, putting them all through college. "She won't listen to me," he told Ben. "I thought maybe she might listen to a doctor. That's why I got her to come in."

Ben put the chart aside and sat down on the table beside her. He marveled at how much the young woman had grown. When he'd left, June had been all arms and legs and pigtails. But he recalled that even then she'd had a knack for figuring out what was wrong with a machine and how to fix it.

"June," he began kindly, "you may not think so, but you're not Superwoman."

June blew out a breath as she shot an exasperated glance at her husband. "I'm not trying to lift the car, Doc, just fix a few things on it. I get antsy sitting on the sidelines," she complained.

"This is the time to shore up your energy," Ben pointed out to her. "Because once that baby's here, trust me, you're going to need it. Babies take up a disproportionate amount of time and energy for their size."

June tossed her head. "Gran was at work in the morning, gave birth to Mom at noon and was back at work by three."

"She was sorting mail," Kevin reminded her. Ursula had told him all about life in the small town when she had been June's age. "And back then the mail plane only came to Hades once a week."

"June, try to take it easy," Ben told her, his voice a little more authoritative. "The cars aren't going anywhere, and Andy and Pete," he referred to the two young men she had working at the shop, "can't learn what to do if you do everything yourself." The expression on his face turned serious. "You don't want anything happening to the baby because you were being stubborn, do you?"

June pressed her lips together and shook her head. "No."

Ben grinned, getting off the table. "Right answer. Okay, now fill me in on everything else." He picked up the chart again. "Any other complaints?"

She sighed, then stuck out her legs in front of her. "Yeah, my feet are swelling."

As she spoke, giving him the details he'd asked for, Ben heard the bell that was mounted over the front door ring twice. It was going to be a long day. But he was looking forward to tonight.

"About time you got home."

The sharp words greeted Heather the moment she opened the front door and walked in. It was as if her mother had waited for her at the window.

In less than a heartbeat, Hannah and Hayley surrounded her and grasped her waist with eager little arms and hands.

Draping an arm around each girl, Heather paused to savor the moment. To her this was what it was all about. Her daughters. This was permanent; this was real. She smiled wryly. The other wasn't real.

Ben Kerrigan was just a dream she was having, a fantasy destined to fade away into the mists. There was no doubt in her mind that he would be out of her life very soon. The next time a whim moved him.

That he'd been attentive, that he'd taken her and the girls out several times, well, that was just something she could remember fondly later. When she was alone again.

Looking up at her mother, Heather put her own

interpretation to Martha Ryan's terse words. "Girls giving you trouble today?"

"No." And then, as if her mother couldn't allow that answer to pass, she added, "No more than usual."

"Then why the sudden delight in seeing me come home?"

Martha pursed her lips, deepening the frown that had become imbedded in her face. "I need help."

Heather looked at her mother warily. "What's wrong, Mother?"

"I can't zip up this damn dress, that's what's the matter," Martha snapped, shifting as much as she was able within the chair.

For the first time since she'd come home, Heather actually looked at her mother, not just her expression or her countenance, but what she was wearing.

It wasn't one of the fleece robes her mother favored, the ones that accentuated the fact that she considered herself a shut-in. Instead Martha Ryan had on her navy-blue dress with the white collar and cuffs. Heather vaguely recalled seeing that dress on her mother when she was a young girl. Heather was surprised that the dress appeared to still fit her mother. She was even more surprised so see that her mother wore it. And that she had makeup on.

After disengaging herself gently from the girls, Heather went over to her mother. Was her mother expecting company? Was she going out again? She felt a smile forming inside her at the thought that her mother was human after all.

"Lean forward," she instructed softly. When her mother obeyed, Heather pulled the zipper all the way up, then gently tucked the dress down so it wouldn't wrinkle. "What's the occasion?"

"You ought to know." Martha's tone was far from chatty or friendly as she straightened again. Her eyes deliberately on her dress, she smoothed out her skirt, saying a few choice things about the effect that life in a wheelchair had on dress fabric.

"If I knew, Mother, I wouldn't ask."

Martha turned her wheelchair around so that she could catch her reflection in the mirror. "They're having a party for him."

Him. Her first thought was of Ben, but her mother didn't even like Ben, so she wouldn't be preparing to go to a party for him. Besides, he would have mentioned something about it when she saw him the other night. "Who's having a party for whom?"

Martha frowned, her eyes narrowing. "That Ike character. For your boyfriend."

Heather was vaguely aware of Ike's custom of throwing parties for newcomers. When Joe was alive, she'd attended several such celebrations. Ike liked to throw parties whenever someone new came to town, or someone decided to return for a visit. Any excuse would do, really. But once Joe was gone, she'd reverted back to her shy state and kept to herself whenever there was any kind of a party. No one really asked questions.

"Ike is having a party?" she echoed.

"For your boyfriend," Martha repeated. "I'm surprised you don't know about it."

She was way too tired to deal with her mother right now. All she wanted was a quick shower and to curl up on the bed, watching some silly children's program with her girls.

"I've been working all day, Mother. And if you're referring to Ben—"

Martha snorted. "Of course I'm referring to Ben. How many boyfriends do you have, girl?"

Heather planted herself firmly before her mother. "By last count, none."

"He was just here the other night." Martha scowled. "That man dump you?" It was more of an accusation than anything else.

Out of the corner of her eye, Heather saw that both Hannah and Hayley were listening to the conversation as if their very existence depended on absorbing every word. She didn't want them getting the wrong idea about what was going on between her and Ben. And she really didn't want them getting attached, although it might already be too late for that. She'd seen how they looked at him, how Hayley even attempted to flirt a little, although she doubted the little girl actually knew what she was doing. As for Hannah, there was a clear case of hero worship in her eyes.

How ironic. Hannah worshipped her father. And so far, with good reason. Because Ben treated them both as if they mattered. As if they were little people. He certainly treated them with more interest and respect than her own mother did.

As for her, he treated her like a friend. A friend he was catching up on life with, nothing more. He hadn't even kissed her again since that first time. If she'd been more than a friend, he would have at least tried again once.

It was almost as if he'd regretted their kiss. Now he was determined to make her understand that there was only friendship between them.

This bothered her. A great deal. But that was her problem, certainly not his. And not any concern of her mother's.

"Mother," she said softly, "that's not the kind of relationship that Ben and I have." She avoided looking at Hannah as she said, "He's a friend."

Rather than the extensive debate she was anticipating, her mother merely shrugged indifferently. "If that's what you want to call it. Here." Her mother held out a necklace to her. "Help me with this."

Heather stared at the single strand. "Your pearl necklace?" She looked up at her mother. It was the one piece of good jewelry her father had given her mother. "You haven't had that on since—"

"Since your no-good father left," Martha completed her thought. "Yes, I know. Just because he was a worthless, no-account is no reason to take it out on the necklace," Martha informed her.

Heather tried to process what was going on. Apparently a leopard *could* change its spots, because this was a completely different woman from the one she'd grown up with. Looking back, her mother had been different now for several weeks. If not for the occasional snapping and displays of ill humor, Heather would have said that someone had kidnapped her mother, leaving a rather even-tempered clone in her place.

And it was all Ursula's doing, Heather thought, and Yuri's cousin, Jan.

However long this lasted—and she had become too much of a realist to believe that it could go on indefinitely—she was grateful.

"Are you going in that?" Martha asked suddenly, turning her wheelchair around sharply and looking her over with that critical expression Heather knew so well.

No one had asked her, and Heather wasn't in the habit of inviting herself to anything. "No, I'm not going at all."

"You're going to play hard to get?" Martha asked incredulously. "With Ben Kerrigan?"

"I thought you hated Ben."

"He's a doctor," Martha pointed out. "I can learn to overlook his shortcomings."

"Mother, if he stays here, Ben's going to be a doctor in a town that's not exactly affluent."

"A doctor's a doctor," Martha replied philosophically.

Heather could only shake her head in wonder.

This woman was *not* her mother. "Whatever this Jan is doing, tell him I approve."

Martha glared at her. "He's not doing anything." But just then the doorbell rang and her mother was transformed from a sour-faced woman to an almost eager-eyed, flustered adolescent.

"Get that!" Martha ordered eagerly.

The closest to the door, Hayley pivoted on her heel and began to yank it open.

"No," Heather ordered, running up to the door. "You're not supposed to open it unless I tell you to."

Hayley frowned. "There's no strangers here, Mama," she told her with an air of authority.

"There are some," Heather told her patiently. "You didn't know grandma's friend Jan until a few weeks ago, did you?" She looked from one face to the other. The girls solemnly shook their heads. "He was a stranger. And Doc Ben, he was a stranger until you were introduced—"

"Give her the object lesson later," Martha insisted, growing visibly more antsy. "Just please get the door."

Please. Now there was a word she hadn't heard her mother use very often.

Stifling a laugh at her mother's poorly concealed zeal, Heather opened the door, ready to greet the miracle workers known as Ursula and company.

The greeting on her lips faded in surprise as the man in the doorway evoked cheers from Hannah and Hayley, who were now flanking her.

Ben grinned back in response.

Chapter Ten

Despite the fact that he had been back a month and their paths had crossed a number of times, Heather still couldn't get used to seeing Ben. Each time was like the first time at the clinic. Tiny shock waves would undulate through her veins, as if an impromptu party was going on inside her body.

Just like now.

It took her a moment to step aside and allow him in.

"Hi." The smile in his eyes, never mind his lips, lit up her house. When he looked at her girls and repeated the greeting with warmth, her heart felt so full.

"Hi!"

"Hi!"

Both girls instantly turned into jumping jacks and surrounded him, their young voices blending into a joyous symphony.

After returning their affection, Ben focused his attention on the one member of the family who had said nothing. "Hello, Mrs. Ryan. You look lovely tonight."

Was it her imagination or did her mother look just the slightest bit flustered by the compliment? But then, the next moment Martha Ryan was once again flying true to form. "Meaning I didn't the last time you came to the house?"

"Lovelier," Ben corrected himself without missing a beat.

With an almost royal nod of her head, Martha appeared pleased at the correction. And placated.

"I'd forgotten just how smooth your tongue can be," Heather murmured to him, low enough for her mother to miss the comment. The vaguest hint of a frown formed on his face, evoking confusion from her. Had she insulted him? Hurt his feelings? "What?"

His eyes held hers just for a moment. She tried to read his thoughts and failed. "Makes me sound like a snake oil salesman."

She *had* insulted him. God, that hadn't been her intention. "I didn't mean—"

Overhearing, Hayley tugged on Ben's jacket to

secure his attention. Her pretty face was puckered in confusion. "What's snake oil?"

"Something that comes in a pretty package but doesn't work," Ben answered simply. He raised his eyes to Heather. Was that what she thought of him? As someone who was always trying to sell people on something that had no value? Did she think of him as being self-centered? Shallow? The thought bothered him.

"You're not in a package." Hayley giggled, covering her mouth as if to keep the sound from erupting.

Ben winked at her, completely winning her heart all over again. "It would have to be a very large package." And then he looked at the other females in the small living room. "I came to invite you ladies to the Salty Dog. Seems they're giving a party in my honor." The last word echoed back at him and he grinned. "Now there's something I never thought I'd hear myself say." He rolled it over again on his tongue. "My honor."

"Like when Mama asks us a question and we gotta answer 'On my honor'?" Hannah asked.

Heather noticed the girl no longer hung back the way she usually did, a prisoner of her own shyness. Since Ben had started paying attention to her, Hannah had begun to bloom.

But he's not going to keep coming around, Heather reminded herself for the umpteenth time. Today, tomorrow, next week, he'll be gone. Just like he was the last time. She drew in her breath, as if already bracing herself. *Don't get used to this. Don't let the girls get used to this.*

"A penny for your thoughts."

Heather jumped, startled. She hadn't realized that Ben had said something to her and had an amused expression on his face. He probably thought she was an empty-headed dolt, incapable of a complex sentence, much less a complex thought.

"Yes," she told him decisively. "I was thinking yes. In answer to your invitation," she added.

To her surprise Ben traced his fingertip along the small, furrowed area between her eyes. "Looked like there was more going on than just that."

Her heart hammered madly. Heather willed herself to remain calm, or at least to look that way. "No." And then she summoned a smile. "A penny doesn't go very far these days."

The grin that unfolded on his lips went straight to her overworked heart. "I'll have to remember that."

Everything in the room faded to a blur. How did he keep *doing* that?

And then the doorbell rang, shattering the moment. And saving her.

"Who's that? Who's that?" Hayley asked, excitement vibrating in her voice.

"Answer it," Martha ordered her daughter, unable to conceal her own excitement.

Before Heather could comply, Ben reached over for the doorknob and opened the door.

This time it was Ursula, Yuri and his cousin, Jan. Glancing at her mother, she saw that at least for the moment, Martha hadn't managed to hide her pleasure. She was smiling.

"What are you doing here, Doc?" Ursula asked, giving Ben the once-over as she walked into the house. "Why aren't you at the party?"

Same old Ursula, Ben thought. The postmistress acted as if everything fell under her purview. It never occurred to her that someone might not want to share their business with her—and the entire town.

"Because I wanted to first stop by here and ask these lovely ladies—" this time both girls giggled "—if they wanted to go to the Salty Saloon with me."

"Of course they want to go with you." Ursula looked at him as if any other conclusion was out of the question. "If I was forty years younger and not being courted by this young stud, here—" she nodded toward Yuri with a wicked grin "—I'd want to go with you."

Jan had moved over toward Martha and now took her hand, kissing it. "Good evening, Mar-ta. You are looking lovely tonight."

Martha sniffed, but she obviously adored the attention and Jan's old-fashioned courtliness. "So I've already been told." As she spoke, she struggled hard to suppress a pleased smile.

"By someone with very good taste, no doubt," Jan asserted. Moving behind her wheelchair, he took hold of the handles. "You are ready?"

"Of course I'm ready," she returned, but only half as gruffly as she ordinarily did. "What are you waiting for? The party will be over before we get there."

"But the guest of honor, he is standing in your house." Jan indicated Ben. "I know you do things differently here, but not that differently, yes?" He looked to Ursula and his cousin for confirmation.

Heather paused to lean over the wheelchair and whisper in her mother's ear. "Can you sheathe your tongue just a little, Mother? You don't want to be driving this one away."

"What I want or don't want is my business, not yours," Martha hissed back at her in what was less than a stage whisper. Even so, her expression was a little uneasy as she twisted around to look at her "driver." Looking down at her, Jan smiled. Relieved, Martha settled back in her chair. Her eyes narrowed just a little as she looked at her daughter. "Well, what are *you* waiting for?" she asked. "Christmas?"

One last bit of hesitation lingered. Heather glanced from Hannah to Hayley, both of whom were bright-eyed. "You girls aren't too tired?"

"The girls'll be fine," Ursula assured her before the chorus of protests could begin. "Matter of fact, when we get there," the woman continued, looking from one small face to the other, "I want you little ones to hang out with me."

"Why?" Hayley asked.

Ursula wrapped one arm around each little girl.

"Because it's been a while since I had little people around me. I've got two grandbabies on the way and I'm out of practice."

Hayley's animated face scrunched. "But they're gonna be littler than us."

"Not for long, honey." Ursula raised her eyes to Heather's. "Not for long," she repeated meaningfully. "Seems like only yesterday, April, Max and June were little like you. And now look." The last sentence was accompanied with a sigh.

"Max?" Hannah echoed, her eyes growing wide. "The sheriff?"

Ursula nodded her head solemnly. "Yes."

"The sheriff was little once, too?" Hannah seemed to have trouble with the concept.

Delighted, Ursula laughed and then gave Hannah a big, warm hug, holding her for a moment to her ample bosom. "See why I love them so much?"

It seemed to Heather that Ursula's rhetorical question was not only addressed to her but to Ben, as well. As if the postmistress was trying to get a message across to both of them.

Heather shifted. It wasn't a message she figured Ben appreciated hearing so she glanced at him uneasily. But if he felt uncomfortable, he gave no indication. His expression was nothing short of genial, as always.

"Can we go, Mama?" Hannah asked. Unlike Hayley, she didn't automatically assume that everything would always go her way. Hannah was her thoughtful one.

Placing her arm around the girl's shoulders, she drew Hannah to her for an abbreviated hug. "I guess, for a little while."

"Great. I've got the four-by-four waiting outside," Ben told her. After having to borrow a car from either Shayne or Sydney, he was glad finally to be behind the wheel of his own vehicle. Heather and her girls had been the first ones he'd taken for a spin.

"Of course you do, silly," Hayley declared, her green eyes dancing. "It's too big to fit in the house."

The simple, innocent observation tickled Ben. "Smart as a whip, these two," he told Heather.

Warning bells went off in her head. The girls enjoyed riding around in Ben's truck way too much. Maybe she needed to ease a separation between them, starting now.

"The car seats are in my car," Heather pointed out to him.

"They can be transferred." He led the way out to his vehicle, which was parked right beside Heather's in the driveway.

"We don't need car seats," Hayley protested as Ben opened the door to Heather's car. "We're big girls."

"And nobody hits anybody with their car." Hannah parroted something she must have overheard.

They'd had this debate before. Heather eyed Ben, expecting him to side with the girls. They both seemed able to twist him around their little fingers whenever they wanted.

But instead, Ben surprised her.

"You do like being safe, right?" He looked from one little girl to the other, and they both nodded. "Well, you just never know when a moose might come running by and decide to butt the car. You'll be safe in your car seat if it ever does." He paused, waiting.

"Okay. We'll sit in the car seats," Hayley reluctantly agreed.

"Yeah, okay," Hannah added in her vote.

Heather's heart ached a little as she saw her older daughter gaze at Ben with adoring eyes.

What would you say, honey, if I told you that was your daddy? What would you both say?

Heather wondered this as her eyes swept over Ben and Hannah. He handily removed first one car seat from her vehicle, then the other, and placed them inside of his. He seemed to care for them as a father would. There was no use thinking about this since she would never tell Ben.

She strapped Hannah in while Ben did the same with Hayley. Out of the corner of her eye, she noticed him checking to see if Hannah's belt was secure. He'd done it, she knew, purely because he hadn't wanted Hannah to feel he was neglecting her. The man had radar when it came to knowing what women wanted. Even short women.

"That seems like a huge waste of time," she commented, referring to the transfer as she climbed into the front passenger seat. "I could have easily followed you in my car."

Securing his own seat belt, Ben started up the engine. He spared her a glance. "Yeah, but then I wouldn't have had you next to me like this. Or the girls in the back seat," he added for good measure, knowing that his every word was being monitored by an audience of two.

Just before he pulled out of the driveway, Ben lightly brushed his hand across her knee, as if to reinforce his point.

Heather did her best to steel herself. She wouldn't let him get to her, she silently swore. Not again. She wasn't going to be left standing alone at the top of the hill, looking down into the lake's waters, thinking her life was over when he left.

The way she had the first time.

Not get to her? a small voice in her head mocked the words, the sentiment. *Too late.*

And then, mercifully, the sound of her girls laughing at something Ben had just said drowned out the voice. For now.

By the time they arrived, the Salty Dog Saloon teemed with people. Ursula and the others had taken off before them and Heather saw that the woman's dark-green vehicle was parked on the very outskirts of the filled-to-capacity lot. She tried to picture her mother inside the establishment. It wasn't easy.

The noise coming from inside the Salty could be heard more than two blocks away. The joyful noise only grew louder as they approached. Glancing in the rearview mirror, she could see her daughters growing progressively more excited. Unlike some of the other children in Hades, Hannah and Hayley had never been to the saloon before. The Salty Dog was more than a hundred years old, originally established by a British expatriate who'd built the place along the lines of an English Pub. Families were just as welcome here as single miners trying to brush away the dust of the day from their souls.

"Will there be games?" Hayley asked, raising her voice to be heard.

"Probably not," Ben guessed. He doubted Heather would let either of the girls try their hands at darts. "But there'll be other kids."

"I want you to stay close to me, girls," Heather cautioned as Ben brought the truck to a stop, parking the vehicle across the street.

"Judging by how packed that place is, they might not have a choice," he commented. Not that there was anything to worry about. Outside of an occasional poacher, and one very determined Native American who periodically destroyed traps and set captured game free, there was next to no crime in Hades. Certainly none that would concern a mother.

Everyone watched out for everyone else here, especially the children.

The second the girls were out of their car seats, they bolted across the street toward the saloon's door.

"Hannah, Hayley," Heather called after them, her voice all but lost in the din.

"Girls!"

Ben's voice was lower than Heather's, but somehow seemed to carry above the noise. The girls stopped in their tracks just shy of the front entrance. Both looked over their shoulders, waiting.

"You're going to have to teach me that trick," Heather said as they hurried across the street to join the girls.

"Looking forward to it." He laughed as he said the words very close to her ear.

She was having some very unplatonic reactions, Heather thought as goose bumps rose and marched along her skin. At the same time a warmth spread itself through her inner core.

"Your mother asked you to stay close," he reminded the girls. Hannah seemed immediately penitent. Hayley just seemed eager. "Okay, girls, you ready?" Two heads nodded vigorously. He pulled open the heavy wooden door. "Let's go in."

"Here he is, the man of the hour," Ike declared the moment Ben entered. He took in the three Kendall females. "Flanked by women as usual. So what else is new?"

Standing at the long bar, Shayne looked at his watch as his brother joined him. "An hour. That's about right. That's all it takes to put Hades behind you. An hour by car. Less by plane."

Ben refused to be baited. The way he saw it, Shayne had a great deal to get off his chest and he deserved every snide comment. Eventually, though, Ben promised himself, his older brother would come around. He had to because this was his home. It had taken him a long time to realize that.

Ben accepted the beer that Ike sent his way along the highly polished mahogany counter. "Trying to get rid of me?" he asked his brother with a laugh.

There was no humor in Shayne's expression as his eyes met Ben's. "Seems to me that there was no trying involved the last time."

Ike leaned over the counter. "Let it go, man," he advised, a steely note underlying the friendly tone of his voice.

"I second the motion," Sydney said, joining her husband and her brother-in-law. She nodded at Heather as she raised her own mug of beer.

Jean Luc, Ike's young, far more soft-spoken cousin, pressed a mug of ale into Heather's hand while Ike's wife presented Hannah and Hayley each with a glass of dark soda pop. The girls looked very happy to have their own drinks, just like the grown-ups.

"To Ben," Ike declared, raising a finely carved

tankard that had been in his family for several generations. "Welcome home."

"For however long that is," Shayne murmured to himself.

Ben caught his brother's words and flashed him a broad grin. "Until you tell me to leave."

They both knew that would never happen. Shayne had done everything in his power to make life easy for Ben to get him to remain in the first place.

"And if I hold you to that?" Shayne raised his eyes now to Ben's.

"I'm counting on it." Ben never flinched, never moved a muscle.

"All right. To my brother, the wandering doctor. Welcome home." Shayne raised his glass this time, sealing the toast.

The last part of the sentiment was echoed many times over. Only Shayne and Heather were left to wonder how long the stay was for this time.

The food served and savored had come courtesy of Lily. The good time came thanks to Ike and the rest of the people crowded in at the Salty.

Heather watched quietly as woman after woman, young, old and in between, stopped to talk and reminisce with Ben. And flirt. What surprised her most was that even when Jennifer Simon tugged on his arm, trying to get him to come away with her to a more private corner of the saloon, Ben never left the table he shared with her and the girls.

A corner jukebox was fed a steady diet of change.

The barely audible music blended pleasantly with the mingling voices. The result was an oddly harmonious blend that evoked a feeling of well-being and belonging for one and all.

Heather noted several times that her mother appeared to be flirting with Jan. Martha Ryan looked younger, happier than Heather could recall ever seeing her. Her mother had certainly never looked this way when she was married. Heather always thought her father had been a saint who had finally been driven away by his wife's moods.

But maybe it hadn't been all one-sided. Maybe there was more to the story. She had no way of knowing. Right now she was glad to see her mother with something other than a frown on her face, her shoulders slumped in abject bitterness and defeat.

As the evening began to wind down and the energy level of her daughters dwindled, Ike's wife, Marta, came over to their table.

"I'm stealing your girls for the night," the woman informed her. "My girls want to have Hannah and Hayley at the house for a sleepover."

"Which means no one sleeps," Ike commented dryly. But he was accustomed to that kind of thing. Five years ago he had taken in his younger sister's infant daughter when Juneau had suddenly died. His own daughter had been born nine months to the day that he and Marta had gotten married. That placed both of his daughters around the same age as Heather's. They were all fast friends.

"Is it all right?" Marta asked, not wanting to push too hard.

"Please, Mama, please," both girls chorused in almost a single voice.

Ben grinned, coming to their aid. "How can you say no to those pleading little faces?" he asked her.

She couldn't.

She didn't.

And as a reward, Heather found herself being smothered with tiny butterfly kisses.

Chapter Eleven

She watched as Hannah and Hayley were gleefully herded off with the LeBlanc girls. It was past her daughters' bedtime and they showed no signs of fatigue as they made their way outside with Marta and their little friends.

Someone got in her way and Heather leaned over in her chair, trying to watch the girls for as long as she physically could.

"They'll be all right."

Ben's voice pulled her away from her concerns and back to the center of the Salty Dog. "What?"

"The girls." He nodded in the general direction they had taken. "They'll be all right."

"How did you know?"

Smiling, he rose and took her hand, coaxing her to her feet. He had a desire to be away from all these people.

"It's written all over your face. First time they've been away from home?" he guessed.

"First time they've been away from me," she corrected. "And me from them," she added softly.

He nodded, guiding her toward the front entrance. "I'd say that it's good for all of you."

With her girls gone for the night and her mother showing no signs of wanting to go home, she supposed this was a good time to catch a little alone time for herself. She couldn't remember the last time that had happened. But now that she was faced with the prospect, it didn't seem all that attractive to her.

She liked having her spaces filled up, she realized. Liked not being alone.

"Is that your professional opinion?" she asked as they edged closer to the door.

"If you like." Holding the door open for her, Ben saw the smile that curved her mouth. Felt himself responding to it. There was something about the woman that still got to him. Just as it had that night. Back then he'd thought it was just a fluke. Now he wasn't so sure. "What?"

She shook her head. "Nothing. Just the way you put it, that's all." Heather pushed her hands deep into her pockets. There had to be a thousand stars in the sky tonight. Summer nights took a long time before they finally arrived, but they were well worth the wait. "I'd like a lot of things."

Taking her hand, Ben crossed the parking lot, heading across the street to where he'd left his vehicle. The party behind him was still going on, but he doubted if anyone would really notice that the "guest of honor" had left. He was just the excuse they'd used to throw a party.

"Such as?"

"Such as a secure future for the girls. I'd like to work a little less and enjoy them a little more before they're all grown-up and think they know better than me."

Heather paused for a second. She was being unusually talkative tonight. Maybe it was the beer she'd had. Granted it didn't have much of a kick, but she wasn't accustomed to drinking at all. Whatever the reason, the words seemed to pour out of her.

"And I'd like for them to know what it's like to have a father." A wistful sigh accompanied her words. "They were just babies when Joe died. Hannah hardly remembers him and I know that Hayley doesn't. He's just a man in a photograph to her."

Reaching his car, Ben turned toward her. "Plenty of men must have asked you." Given the scarcity of women in the area, he found himself wondering why she hadn't married again.

She shrugged, looking away. "There've been a few."

Taking her chin in his hand, he gently brought her face toward his. "But?"

But none of them were you. "I'm waiting to feel the earth move. To experience an eclipse of the sun. To stand in the center of the aurora borealis." Was that so much to ask? To have that wonderful rush again? More than that, to feel as if every day was a wonderful gift?

He couldn't quite reconcile what she was telling him to what he knew had already taken place in her life. But then, he supposed everyone was different. Still, he had to ask. "Is that what happened with Joe?"

"Joe?" She laughed softly, shaking her head. The earth had never moved for her with him. Her pulse hadn't even rushed. Not once. Not even when she willed it. "No. Joe was a very sweet, kind man who just came along at the right time."

She had completely lost him. "The right time?"

Heather pressed her lips together. She was very close to telling him the truth. To saying that she'd suddenly found herself pregnant and had been desperate, just when Joe had made his feelings for her known. The words, the admission, hovered on her tongue.

"I needed a knight in shining armor. He was a miner covered in coal dust, but his heart was in the right place."

Ben looked at her for a long moment. "Why did you need a knight in shining armor, Heather?"

No, she couldn't do it. Couldn't tell him and see anger or, worse, pity in his eyes. Hannah was her secret and would remain that way.

She sighed. "I just did, that's all." Summoning a wide smile, she changed subjects. "So, I hear that you just moved into the Logan place. How's that going for you?"

Shayne had been surprised when Ben had told him about buying the old place. But he needed to be on his own. Needed to be something other than the little brother. This was a step in the right direction, even if it represented a hell of an undertaking.

"Needs a lot of work. A lot of cleaning," he told her, leaning back against his car. Joshua Logan had moved his family to Utah and left the house in the hands of a realty company domiciled in Anchorage. The man who ran the general store doubled as a real estate agent, and he had set the paperwork in motion for him. The place had become officially his as of yesterday. "Place hasn't been lived in for five years—except for a family of squirrels."

"Better that than a family of bears." They were not without their wild animals in this part of the state. More than once, bears, deer and moose had wandered into town, looking for food.

He nodded. Impulse nudged him, but he debated a couple of seconds before finally asking, "Would you like to see it?"

The question caught her by surprise. Stalling

for time, she smiled. "What? The family of squir-rels or the dust?"

"The squirrels moved out, and the dust situation is getting under control. Sydney and the kids came by yesterday while I was at the clinic, got a good start making the place a real home." Shayne had turned out to be one lucky man, he thought. Sydney was a very special lady. But then, so was Heather.

He brushed a hair back from her face, fighting the urge to kiss her. Knowing if he did, he'd have an audience. People would come pouring out of the Salty to watch. "I thought I might ask your opinion about some things."

It was a bad idea; she knew that. She should just tell him to take her home and that she'd accept a rain check.

Still she heard herself saying, "All right."

He smiled as he opened the passenger door for her.

The Logan place wasn't far from the lake. Sitting beside Ben as she traveled, she sifted through a host of memories. Memories she both welcomed and tried to keep at bay. They made her feel vulnerable.

Unlike many of the structures around town, the Logan place was more cabin than house. The whole scene was very rustic, with the trees flanking the cabin and the lake at its back.

After getting out of the truck, Heather walked up to the front door and turned the knob, only to find that it wouldn't give. She looked over her shoulder at Ben, a silent query in her eyes. For the most part, the doors in Hades remained unlocked.

"Habit I got into in Seattle," he confessed. It took him a second to find the right keys. He unlocked the door, then pushed it open so she could enter first. "Not that I have anything worth taking," he commented. There was a light switch right by the door. He tried it, as he had the night before, but nothing happened. "Looks like they still haven't gotten around to turning on the electricity."

He'd asked to have it turned on when he'd signed the papers that began the process of making the property his. But things in Hades moved at their own pace. No one was in a hurry.

Leaving the door open, he used the moonlight to illuminate the room and guide him to the table. A hurricane lamp sat in the center. Ben lit it and then stood back. The light cast was minimal, but intimate.

He smiled as he turned around to look at Heather. "I guess you can get a better idea in the daytime."

"Not necessarily." Wrapping her hands around her forearms, Heather slowly looked around, taking measure of the surroundings. His whole existence seemed crowded into the one front room. There was a fireplace to one side and a bed directly opposite. Several partially open boxes lined the walls. "It's deceptive." She turned around to face him. "Seems smaller from outside."

Seemed pretty small on the inside to him, he

thought. But he was pleased that she seemed to like it. "I think ultimately I might need more room, but for now this'll do."

He was talking about moving. She was thinking about it in terms of expanding.

"You could always add on," she suggested. "I hear Kevin Quintano is pretty handy when it comes to building things." Lily had told her about the nursery her brother had built for her and the one he was still working on for June. She had a feeling that if the woman's older brother had been lacking in skills, Lily would have added that into the story. "And there's always George."

"Mayfield?" he asked and she nodded. "Is he still around?" George Mayfield had been the town handyman when he was a kid, Ben recalled. The man had a love affair with wood. "I haven't seen him since I got back. Didn't see him tonight."

"He was there," she assured him. Humor played along her lips. "But then, you might have missed seeing him because your vision was obstructed for most of the evening."

He gazed at her. Feelings he had been dealing with all evening began coming to the fore. "Yes, I know."

She shook her head. "Nothing's changed. You still have hot-and-cold-running women coming your way."

"Oh." It suddenly dawned on him what she was referring to. "I wasn't thinking about the people who stopped by."

Women, she thought. The *women* who had stopped by. It seemed to her as if every female in Hades had come by his table to talk to him, at least for a few moments. "Then what were you thinking of?"

He would have thought that was rather obvious. "You."

Heather stared at him, floored. Was he teasing her? "Me?"

"Yes. You're the one who was blocking my vision all night." And she was the one who was filling it now, just with her presence. Ben could feel desire stirring within him.

She held her hands out as if to display herself. "I tip the scales at one-fourteen."

"Figuratively," he told her, his mouth curving. "You were blocking my vision figurative." She hadn't been the prettiest woman there tonight. And certainly not the most aggressive. And yet all he could think about was Heather. "Because all I saw tonight was you."

"Even with Margaret Taylor's augmented breasts in your face?"

The young woman, who had made no secret of the fact that she was more than a little pleased that Ben was back and that she intended to land him for herself this time, had been a repeat visitor to the table. She was dressed in a black T-shirt and matching jeans that someone had painted on her and had tried her damnedest to draw Ben away from the table. Margaret would have been thrilled to death to be here with him like this.

As if I'm not.

That was just the trouble. She was. She was thrilled to be here, thrilled to be anywhere with him. Anticipation and hope elevated her heart rate. Telling herself to get a grip fell on deaf ears.

"Even then. Actually," he deadpanned, "I never noticed they were augmented."

"Then, doctor, I suggest you get an eye exam and have yourself fitted for glasses immediately because bats see better than you do."

Crossing to the door, he closed it. "Maybe the sight never registered because I had something better to look at."

The soft click the door made echoed throughout her body. She was aware of everything, of the very air around her, and warmth as adrenaline surged through her veins.

"Smooth as ever," she murmured for a second time that evening. Her mouth curved as she remembered his comment. "What kind of snake oil would you like to sell me?"

Somehow, the distance between them had disappeared. He wasn't at the door any longer but right beside her. Blocking out everything else.

"Nothing," he answered, combing his fingers through her hair. Framing her face. "I don't want to sell you anything. But I would like to kiss you."

"Are you asking my permission?" She was surprised she could talk, since her heart had just leaped into her throat.

The smile on his lips went straight to that lodged heart. "Something like that."

She took a breath, afraid of suffocating if she didn't. "You have changed."

When Lila had walked out on him, he didn't think that he could ever feel again, ever allow himself to feel again. Now he realized that "allowing" had nothing to do with it. Things evolved without permission. And all he could do was hang on for the ride and hope not to crash and burn at the end.

This woman from his past was doing things to him that he wouldn't have dreamed possible. "For the better, I'd like to think."

"That would be trying to improve on perfection."

She had never struck him as being sarcastic, yet he couldn't see how she could seriously utter the comment. But Heather wasn't the type to offer empty flattery, either. She was as different from Lila as sunlight was from artificial lighting.

"So far from perfection that I can't even find my way back," he told her softly.

All sorts of delicious things happened inside of her. And everything felt as if it was holding its breath. Waiting. "Try."

"Yes, ma'am."

Ben lowered his mouth to hers.

At first, it felt like slow motion. As if the fire taking hold of her, spreading to all her limbs, progressed an inch at a time, taking her prisoner.

Who was she kidding? She was already a

prisoner, capitulating the second he had *touched* her, never mind kissed her. Heather could feel her head spinning, could feel the darkened room fading away. There was nothing and no one but him.

She'd been waiting for this, waiting ever since Ben had kissed her on her doorstep. Her body primed, recalling another evening, by the lake. When she had given him her virginity and he had given her the dreams that saw her through to this day.

That, and Hannah.

And now they were back at the lake. Back to the same magical time. Yes, she'd grown, yes, she had two children, but the need that had been there then still lived within her.

It escalated, demanding attention. Demanding release. Heather wrapped her arms around his neck, bringing her body against his.

Bringing her soul to him, as well.

The kiss deepened, fueled by a hunger she hadn't realized she had. A hunger that had never once come close to being sated the times that she and Joe had made love. With Joe lovemaking had always been a pleasant experience, but the earth remained where it was, and, if it had been necessary, she could have easily done long division in her head. She never lost sight of where she was or who she was. Not even once.

It was different with Ben.

With Ben, just kissing him made the room burn

away in layers, leaving her free-falling in space, where there was no beginning, no end. Only exhilaration.

As she felt herself being consumed with desire, as passions beat wild, filmy wings within her, she didn't want things progressing in slow motion anymore. Didn't want to languidly take her time, to enjoy every scrap like some newfound treasure. She wanted the shooting stars, the wildness. She wanted it all.

Her body sang as it gave itself up to the grasp of passion.

He realized this was like his first time with her. Like trying to hold a shooting star in his hand. She made his blood surge, made him want to ravage her, to pleasure her, to be the best that he could. He wanted to be all things for her, with her.

The force of the kiss overwhelmed him, urging him to move forward until suddenly he had her against the wall, trapped between it and his body. Every part of him filled with anticipation as the soft contours of her body pressed against his, forming almost a seal.

A hunger came out of nowhere, exploding within him not by increments but by a geometric progression. One moment it was a speck, the next, it filled all of him. He ran his hands over her curves, remembering the last time. Wanting her.

Heather moaned against his mouth. It was all he needed. He felt the temperature of his blood rise another ten degrees.

Clothes began to disappear, as did judgment.

Led by instincts and needs, they made their way to the bed against the wall. Whether he took her or she him, he didn't know, didn't care. All he knew was that they were lying there together and that he could more easily familiarize himself with every single inch of her.

Desire drummed impatient fingers, demanding release. It was all he could do to hang on a little longer. Because he wanted to take in the taste of her. To lose himself in the softness, the scent, the passion of her.

The way he had the first time.

Her figure was rounder, more supple, and yet still as delicate as it had been then. She was a woman now, a woman who had given birth to two children, and yet, her body was firm, soft, inviting. Giving. His hands swept over every contour even as his mouth sampled, tasted, suckled, in an attempt to get his fill of her.

It seemed like a hopeless task.

Heather twisted and turned into his touch, glorying in the way his clever fingers ignited her inner fire. He made her body sing. He made her body want.

He was making her crazy.

Lightning kept shooting through her veins, as if each area he touched exploded in bouquets of ecstasy. One after the other, climaxes rattled through her body. Every movement of his hand brought forth more. She couldn't get enough, even as she gasped for breath, exhausted and insatiable at the same time. Fearful that it would end just as abruptly as it had begun.

Fearful that she would never feel this way again.

She had no doubt that this was an isolated incident and that there would be no repeat event tomorrow or the day after that or the day after that. He was going with the moment. Tomorrow, someone else would be in his arms. Someone prettier, more desirable, someone who had more to give.

But never someone who loved him more than she did.

Even now, living in the moment, she could feel an ache forming in her heart.

Heather banished it. She needed to enjoy this, to savor this, to commit it to memory the way she had the first time. Because she could go for years on a single memory; she'd already proven that to herself. Each time she lay beside Joe, it was Ben she remembered. Ben she summoned to mind.

Ben she made love with, not Joe. She supposed that made her guilty of adultery in her heart. Because she loved a phantom lover who was never there.

But he was now.

When he had done all he could, held himself back as long as he was humanly able, Ben gathered her to him. With his knee, he spread her legs beneath him and then slipped into her. The gasp of pleasure echoed in his head. The swell of her breasts against his chest as Heather took in a deep breath ignited him, and the rhythm began. He kept it going as long as he could, accelerating it ever faster until finally he was swept over the top.

Taking her with him.

The descent occurred without his noticing it. He was too aware of the sensation of holding her to him. Too aware of holding on to the moment.

Chapter Twelve

The hurricane lamp on the table sent out dark-gold glows of light that cast their shadows on the wall, melding their two forms together as closely as they had been moments earlier.

Ben kissed the top of her head, reluctant to release her. Reluctant to release the moment. For the first time in a very long time he felt at peace. As if he belonged.

Funny how life kept not turning out the way you planned. He smiled to himself. "I really didn't have this in mind when I invited you over, you know," he said, his words gently ruffling her hair.

Heather's eyes danced as she looked at him. "Yeah, you did."

Ben sifted a strand of her hair through his fingers, thinking how silky it felt. How silky she felt. And how much he wanted her again.

"Maybe, just a little."

And I wanted you a lot. But that's the way it always was. She made the most of it.

"It's okay." Drawing away from him, she sat up on the bed, ready to rise. She did her best to sound blasé. There had to have been scads of women in his life back in Seattle. "So, I'll meet you at the lake seven years from now."

The statement was a little too glib for him. This wasn't Heather. This wasn't the woman he'd just made love with.

Catching her wrist, Ben pulled her back to him. "How about now?"

She tumbled back onto the bed and stared at him. "Now?"

"Yes." His smile pulled her in. "What are you doing now?"

Loving you. Heather nodded toward the scattered clothing a few feet away on the floor. "I was about to get dressed."

He did his best to look as if he was seriously considering her words. "You sure you want to do that? I'd only have to undress you again."

He wanted her again. Heather allowed her body to relax. Allowed herself to enjoy the moment. For whatever reason, there'd been a stay of execution.

The bubble hadn't burst yet, and she'd been given a little more time to enjoy him.

She lay down next to him. "Exactly what did you have in mind?"

Ben grinned as he felt his body heating. Hardening. Felt a rush beginning within him all over again. "I'll think of something."

It wasn't difficult, he mused, slipping his arms around her again. Not when all his thoughts began and ended with Heather. The light from the hurricane lamp melded their shadows together again.

The throng of patients that showed up daily at the clinic had thinned down somewhat. People had stopped coming by because they were curious to see if the stories about Ben's return were true. The eligible female population of Hades had, for the most part, ceased to make up nonexistent ailments in order to snag a few private moments with the good-looking and only unattached doctor in the area. Their attendance had dropped off when they discovered that they had to endure a long wait for only five minutes of professional time.

With an instinct for self-preservation, Ben had gotten very good at spotting the women with genuine complaints and those who fabricated symptoms and ailments in order to see him.

After a siege of almost eight weeks, the numbers at the clinic became more manageable and life returned to business as usual. Ben wasn't the only one to notice or to breathe a secret sigh of relief.

Picking up the chart that listed the appointments scheduled for that day, Shayne scanned the page. "I think your groupies are finally resigning themselves to seeing you in your off-hours." He glanced in Ben's direction as he returned the chart to Alison's desk.

Finishing the glazed doughnut that represented his breakfast, Dr. Jimmy Quintano dusted off his fingers.

"You say that as if it's a good thing." He dropped his crumpled napkin into the wastepaper basket beside Alison's desk. "Personally, I liked seeing some of Hades's lovelier residents stroll through the office, looking as if they'd all been moonstruck."

Alison walked in from the rear of the building, a giant mug of coffee clutched between her hands. "I bet April took another view of that."

Jimmy gave his younger sister his best reproving look. "And who told her about that?"

They both knew that he'd never been happier since he'd left his roving bachelor days behind him. "Me. And I'd do it again in a heartbeat." She paused to take a long sip of the inky liquid before setting the mug down on her desk. "Now if you'll excuse me, I have some charts to put away." Picking up the two folders that had belonged to patients who had come in after hours, Alison ducked out of the room.

"How about you?" Shayne asked, turning toward his brother.

They still had a few minutes before officially opening, although the waiting room was already full. For once, Shayne decided to take his time. Ben's answer was important to him. In the last few weeks, he'd been forced to reassess his opinion of his brother. Ben appeared to be earnest about atoning for his past transgressions. Earnest about making a life for himself here. But Shayne had been burned more than once by his brother. Somewhere deep in his soul, he kept waiting for a shoe to drop.

"How are you dealing with the drop-off of adoring throngs?"

"Just fine," Ben replied with no hesitation. His eyes met his brother's. "I'm here to practice medicine, not to date."

Shayne nodded thoughtfully, as if still reserving judgment on the validity of that statement. "Speaking of dating, you've been seeing a lot of Heather Kendall."

Out of the corner of his eye, Ben saw Jimmy lean back against the desk, making no secret of the fact that he was listening. "Are you spying on me, Shayne?"

Shayne's broad shoulders rose and fell beneath his white coat. "You live in Hades. Very little of what any of us do can be kept a state secret. Not with Ursula Hatcher around."

"Clever woman, Ursula," Jimmy volunteered.

Both Kerrigan brothers turned to look at him. They waited, but there was no follow-up to the cardiologist's off-handed observation.

"Okay," Shayne said, crossing his arms, "I'll bite. Why is Ursula clever?"

A fondness entered his voice as Jimmy began to speak about his grandmother-in-law. Short on extended family himself, he, like the rest of his siblings, thought very highly of the lively older woman. They all regarded her like the grandmother they never had. For them, more than the Yearlings, who were her actual grandchildren, Ursula could do no wrong.

"Well, for one thing, she found a way to kill two birds with one stone." Jimmy could see that Ben and Shayne were still waiting to be enlightened. "She got Yuri's cousin involved with someone and managed to win a bet at the same time."

The latter was out of left field. "A bet? What kind of bet?" Ben wanted to know.

Jimmy laughed. "She bet me that she could bring Heather's mother around. That she could get the woman to do something other than look bitter and spend her days complaining. Martha Ryan's one of my patients," he explained to Ben. "I've been treating her for a myriad of supposed heart ailments ever since I got here."

"She has a bad heart?" Ben asked. Heather had never mentioned that, but then, she wasn't the kind to complain, and when they were together, they didn't exactly waste time talking about her mother.

Jimmy shook his head. "No more than anyone else her age. What she has is an underused heart.

And imagined chest pains. She's had Heather rush her in here a number of times since I've been in Hades. Each time, the woman swore she was having a heart attack. I'd check her over." He shrugged. "No heart attack. Just a bid for attention. I mentioned it to Ursula and Ursula said that if the woman had something to take her mind off her solitude, maybe it would do her some good. She had Yuri send for Jan."

This was news to Ben. He wondered what Heather would say if she knew all this had been arranged. Probably send Ursula roses, he thought with a smile. "He didn't just arrive here for a vacation?"

Jimmy gave him a penetrating look. "Would you come to Hades for a vacation?"

"You did," Alison reminded him, walking back to her desk now that the folders had been put away.

Jimmy turned around to face her. "That was different. I came here to see you. I called my visit a vacation because it seemed less emotional that way."

Alison grinned. "And we all know how unemotional you are."

"How long is Jan planning on staying here?" Ben asked. He could foresee some really hard times ahead once Martha was alone again.

Jimmy thought for a moment before he answered. "According to Ursula, Yuri said his cousin was coming for three weeks."

Ben glanced at the calendar on the wall, although

there was no real need. "It's been almost two months," he pointed out.

Jimmy laughed. "Yeah, I know. Seems that we've got milder temperatures than he's used to in Russia." He added, "And from what I gather, Jan really does like Heather's mother. The man's thinking of making Hades his permanent home."

"Sounds good to me," Ben commented. Having her mother in a good mood had certainly taken a burden off Heather's shoulders. And the thought of her shoulders brought his mind around to the way she'd looked the other night in his cabin. Ursula had stopped by with Yuri and Jan and he had taken the opportunity to whisk Heather away for a few hours.

A few hours of ecstasy.

Shayne glanced at his watch. They were now officially open for business. "If you ladies are finished talking," he looked from one doctor to the other, "we have a roomful of patients to see."

Jimmy looked at Ben. "Has he always been this bossy, or is it just me?"

Ben laughed. "Yes to both."

Shayne turned around to make a retort, but it was cut short by the sound of the front door slamming against the opposite wall. The sounds of a commotion immediately followed in the waiting room. A child wailed fearfully.

One voice rose above the rest.

"I need help."

Ben felt his heart slam against his rib cage.

Heather.

He hurried over to the door that led out into the waiting room, but Shayne was already ahead of him.

More than a few of the patients were out of their seats, surrounding a very pale-looking, trembling Heather. In her arms, wrapped in a dark-blue blanket, was her firstborn, unconscious and bleeding. Hayley was right next to her, holding tightly onto her skirt and sobbing as loudly as if she were the one who was hurt.

"I didn't mean it, I didn't mean it," the little girl cried over and over again.

Shayne cut through the crowd. "What happened?" he asked Heather.

"She fell off the roof." Even as Heather told him, she could hardly believe what she was saying. This kind of thing just didn't happen, not to her babies. She was always so careful, always laying down the rules for them. But this time Hannah, her obedient Hannah, hadn't listened to the rules.

"The roof?" Shayne echoed incredulously. Anger creased his brow.

"I dared her," Hayley sobbed, her voice muffled against the folds of Heather's black and white skirt. "I called her a baby and said even baby birds fly. So she said she could, too. She did it so I wouldn't call her a baby anymore. I'm sorry. I'm sorry."

Shayne looked at Heather, who could only shake her head. The details of what happened were muddied. She hadn't gotten a clear story herself. When her mother had called the restaurant, all she had managed to get out were the words that Hannah had been hurt. Heather vaguely remembered dropping the phone and rushing out. She didn't remember the drive home.

When she got there, less than ten minutes after the call, she'd found the girl lying in the front yard, hardly breathing and unconscious. Hayley was huddled against the house, crying.

Her mother was just about to summon Jan to pick up Hannah since she couldn't manage to do that herself.

Heather remembered snapping something at her mother. It was the first time she'd ever done that. But cold panic had seized her heart. She'd wrapped Hannah in a blanket, then placed her in the back seat of her car and driven to the clinic as fast as she could. Hayley had all but thrown herself into the car as she was pulling out. She'd had no choice but to bring her, as well.

"Let me handle this," Ben said.

His older brother eyed him uncertainly. Shayne was the one who always took charge in these cases. "I don't think—"

"Shayne, please." Ben struggled to sound dispassionate. "I'm trained in emergency pediatric care."

Making up his mind, Shayne stepped back. "All right, go ahead. I'll be your backup."

Very carefully Ben took the still child from Heather's arms. "Alison, get the main exam area ready."

The main exam area was larger than the other rooms. It doubled as an operating room whenever necessary. This was where they performed minor surgeries and whatever had to be done before a patient could go to Anchorage General for more intensive care.

Heather stiffened. The main exam area was where they had brought Joe when they'd dug him out of the cave-in. Tears sprang to her eyes. The room had seen death. But it had also seen life, she reminded herself fiercely. And Hannah was going to be all right. She *had* to be.

As Ben began to walk away with her daughter, Heather shadowed his steps quickly with Hayley still clinging to her. Ben turned just before he entered the room. Heather's face was ashen.

"You need to stay out here, Heather," he told her gently.

A sob tore at her throat. "She's my baby, Ben. I just can't abandon her."

He wanted to put his arms around her. To tell her that it was going to be all right even though he couldn't tender such guarantees. But Hannah's needs outweighed Heather's and he had to think of the child first.

"You're not abandoning her. You're allowing me to do my job. I'll let you know how she's doing as soon as there's something to know," he promised. He looked down at the sobbing child clinging to Heather's skirt. "Hayley." He made himself sound stern in order to break through her sobs. "Look after your mother."

The little girl nodded solemnly, using the back of her hand to wipe away her own tears. Letting go of Heather's skirt, she took hold of her mother's hand instead. "C'mon, Mama." She led her toward a chair. The crowd parted around them. "We can wait here."

Heather felt as if her very heart had been ripped out of her chest.

"She's lost a lot of blood," Ben told Shayne as the latter entered the main exam room less than five minutes later.

Jimmy, wearing surgical livery, jerked his thumb toward the front of the clinic. "I've got a roomful of volunteers. Say the word and they'll start rolling up their sleeves."

"Might not be a bad idea," Ben agreed. "Type her," he told Alison.

They didn't have to take the time to do that. "Her mother can donate a pint or two," Shayne said, beginning to leave.

But Ben shook his head. "Heather's got a cold. If we do a transfusion, the blood is going to have to come from someone else."

Shayne agreed with Ben's assessment. Heather had sounded nasal, but he'd just assumed that was because she was crying. "I've got everybody's blood type on file," he told his brother. "Shouldn't be a problem finding matches for Hannah."

Alison had already made a smear of Hannah's blood and was hurrying into the lab in order to type it.

"Shouldn't be," Ben echoed, looking at the still child on the table. Despite all of his training, a feeling of helplessness pervaded through him. He struggled to hold it at bay.

She's going to be all right, he promised. Whether he was promising himself or an absent Heather, or even the little girl on the table, he didn't know. But it was a promise he fiercely meant to keep.

Hannah's blood was AB positive. Five of the patients in the waiting room who matched the blood type were well enough to volunteer a pint of their blood.

Surgery was performed as soon as Ben had X-rays to apprise him of the extent of the internal damage. He would have preferred conducting the operation in a hospital, but airlifting Hannah would take time—time they might not have to spare. Despite the X-rays, he wasn't a hundred percent certain what he would find. An MRI would have given him far greater insight, but they didn't have one of those machines on hand.

Maybe a fund-raiser was in order. One conducted in Seattle amid the people he used to rub elbows with, he thought.

But all that was in the future. Right now the only thing that mattered was getting Hannah to open up her big green eyes and look at him again.

And smile at him again, he added.

* * *

There was a clock on the wall opposite where she sat. Every time she looked at it, she could have sworn the hands had remained glued in place. Heather had never known time to move so slowly, even as her heart raced within her chest.

Everyone was being very kind. Jimmy had sent for Ursula. Yuri and his cousin had been dispatched to stay with Martha Ryan, who blamed herself for the accident. Ursula had come to the clinic to console and comfort Heather, giving her a much-needed shoulder to lean on.

Heather couldn't remember the last time she had been able to lean on anyone. Accustomed to braving everything on her own, she at first resisted the woman's efforts but found herself caving very quickly.

Though she did her best not to cry, it was difficult not to as she poured out her fears to the postmistress. Ursula merely listened, stroking Heather's hair and letting her unburden herself. Her oldest granddaughter, April, Jimmy's wife, had come with her to take Hayley away. April took the little girl to Marta's where the latter's daughters distracted Hayley, keeping her mind off what was happening at the clinic.

And still time dragged by as if each second had been dipped in molasses, then mounted on the back of an arthritic slug.

"I hear he's a damn fine doctor," Ursula told her

after she'd sighed again. "Like his brother," she added. "But of the two, Jimmy says that Ben is the more skilled surgeon." Ursula patted her shoulder. "He'll take care of your little girl."

Heather raised her head from the woman's ample bosom. Her eyes were swollen from crying. "He's not a miracle worker."

"Miracles come in all sizes and shapes, honey. They don't all involve moving mountains. Don't go selling him short just yet," Ursula cautioned. She patted Heather's hand. "You have to believe," she told her seriously. "Believe with all your heart."

She was about to say something else, but she stopped abruptly when she saw the rear door open. Ben came out, removing his surgical mask as he walked.

Heather was on her feet like a shot, but her legs wouldn't work, wouldn't carry her to him. She was afraid to ask. Afraid to breathe.

"Hannah sustained a number of broken bones— two cracked ribs, her right arm and wrist—and her liver and spleen were bruised. But she came through the operation like a trooper," he told her proudly.

Her poor baby. "Is she awake? Can I see her?"

"Not yet," he told her, answering her first question, "that's going to take some time." And then he smiled, more relieved than she could possibly know that he could say this to her. "But she's going to be all right and of course you can see her."

"Oh God, thank you." Dissolving into a storm of

tears, Heather threw her arms around his neck. "Thank you."

"She's a strong little girl," he told her above the cheers of the other patients in the waiting room. They were all one big family when it came to things like this, and one of their own had just been spared.

"I knew that," Heather murmured against his neck before she sobbed again.

Inside his office, Shayne pulled out a file from the back of the bottom drawer of his file cabinet. Having given in to Alison's insistence, he had allowed his active files to be input on the computer. In the bottom drawer, he kept the files belonging to the handful of people who had died before Alison had a chance to cajole him into getting a computer to keep track of his patients.

And that was where he kept Joe Kendall's folder.

Holding it now, he flipped it open. Joe Kendall had died in this clinic despite all of his best efforts to save the man. The wounds the miner had sustained in Hades's last major cave-in had been too extensive, too massive. Joe never stood a chance. Even so, he hadn't given the man up without a fight.

Joe had lost over two pints of blood by the time they'd found him and brought him to the clinic. The first thing he'd done after stopping the bleeding was to start a transfusion going.

Shayne looked at the page where Joe's blood type had been entered. Something had been gnawing away at him ever since Ben had told him the little girl's blood type.

He frowned.

Joe's blood type had been O.

Chapter Thirteen

They were running behind more than usual at the clinic.

Shayne had never believed in roller-skate medicine, where the physician would look in on a patient and quickly treat a symptom rather than take the time to get as much information as possible and find out the real problem. A credit to multitasking, Alison ran the technical end of the office as well as performing her nursing duties. She usually scheduled four patients an hour per doctor. But a great many times the visits ran over the allotted fifteen minutes, making them fall behind. With Hannah's emergency surgery tying up both Ben and Jimmy for the better part of two hours, they were running about three hours behind.

Shayne was picking up the slack wherever he could. This frenetic pace brought back memories.

"Seems like old times, doesn't it?" Alison commented as she crossed another name off the schedule. Marianne Anderson was just exiting through the outer door, a supply of allergy medication in her purse.

Shayne made a last notation in Marianne's chart, then set it down. All their exam rooms were filled. "Reminds me that the 'old' days were not always so good," he responded.

He'd been running on empty for a while now.

There'd been no time for lunch and, more important, no time to talk to Ben the way he wanted to. When Ben wasn't busy with the patients in the waiting room, he was looking in on Hannah. By Shayne's count—and it could have been more— Ben did that on the average of five times an hour.

He'd heard Heather tell his brother, "If you charged by the hospital visit, I wouldn't be able to afford you." There had been gratitude shimmering along with the tears in her eyes.

"Don't worry about the costs," Ben had told her.

At least his brother was no longer in it for the money, Shayne thought, picking up the chart that went with room two. That was something. As for himself, much to his late ex-wife's anger, he had never been in it for the money. It had always been, first and foremost, about the patients.

But Ben's philosophy had been to become a doctor and advance himself first. That didn't detract from his skill as a doctor, but it did take away from the kind of person he was. Or had been.

With all his heart, Shayne wanted to believe that Ben had had some kind of epiphany while in Seattle. That his brother had suddenly discovered that life needed more substance to have real meaning. But he just didn't know if that was true. And the information he'd found out this morning just pushed the question of his brother's character further into the undefined, gray area.

Suppressing a sigh, Ben made his way to room two.

Finally the last patient had left.

Shayne had let Jimmy go home to his wife over an hour ago. He made April leave shortly thereafter. He carried on without them. The doors of the clinic were never locked while he was there. He never turned anyone away, so the Closed at 5 O'Clock sign rarely saw any real use. With luck, they finished by six o'clock. Usually later.

It was after seven-thirty.

He knew Sydney would be forgiving as she told him that he worked too hard. He could always depend on Sydney. If there'd been a life before her, he couldn't remember it. After wearily stripping off the white lab coat he wore, Shayne hung it on the other side of his door, then went to find Ben. As anticipated, his little brother was in the operating room with Hannah. The little girl had been floating in and out of consciousness all afternoon. He and Ben both felt it was better that way for the time being. It allowed her to heal without being subjected to the pain that accompanied recovery from a surgery.

Shayne noted Heather had hardly moved since she'd positioned herself beside Hannah's bed shortly after the operation had been completed. She just sat there, holding Hannah's hand in both of hers. And praying.

Ben glanced up at him as he entered.

"Can I have a word with you?" Shayne asked softly.

Ben nodded, slowly withdrawing from the room, as if moving any faster would have some sort of disruptive effect on Hannah and her mother. Easing the door shut, he turned toward his brother. It had been touch-and-go for a while. Tension still danced through him, but to the casual observer, he made himself seem calm and at ease.

"I'm going to stay here tonight," he told Shayne. "Watch Hannah to make sure everything's going well. I was going to have her transferred to Anchorage General in the morning but Heather insists she doesn't want any other doctor attending Hannah except for me." A rueful expression came over his features. "I don't have privileges at Anchorage General yet." Signing up with the hospital hadn't been a priority. Now he wished he had.

Privileges meant that a physician was allowed to use a hospital's facilities whenever he needed to have his patients stay there overnight. Both Jimmy's and Shayne's names were on the hospital roster, allowing them access to Anchorage General's state-of-the-art equipment.

"I can fly her in for an MRI tomorrow to make sure nothing was missed," Shayne offered. His small Cessna was always gassed up and ready to take off for just such emergencies. "You and Jimmy can double up on patients until I get back." They could discuss that further tomorrow, as the need arose. Right now he had something more pressing to address. "Listen, that's not what I wanted to talk to you about."

Ben stiffened. He knew that tone. Something was in the offing that, more than likely, he wasn't going to like. He stopped walking and crossed his arms. Whatever it was, he wanted to take it standing up. "Go ahead."

"Before you left town the last time—" Shayne began.

Ben anticipated what was coming next. Exhaustion and extreme concern turned his patience into a sopping-wet tissue, easily torn.

"Damn it, Shay, what do I have to do to prove to you that I'm here for good?" he demanded, struggling to keep his voice low. "That I'm not the same person I was seven years ago?"

Shayne's expression never changed. It was unreadable. "Well, for one thing, you might try letting me finish my sentences."

Ben blew out an angry breath, getting himself under control. "All right, go ahead."

"Before you left town the last time," Shayne began again, "was Heather one of your conquests?"

Ordinarily Ben had never been quick to anger. But after the day he'd had, his patience was in short supply. He didn't like being judged and didn't care for any disrespect given to the women he'd been with at the time. On their behalf more than his, he took offense.

"None of them were 'conquests,' Shayne," he informed his brother, his voice low and steely. "That's not how it was, and if you thought that something so low drove me, that all I wanted was to 'conquer' women, to put notches on a headboard or a belt, then I guess you never really knew me at all."

Shayne frowned. "You're not answering my question, Ben. I'll rephrase it," he said tersely. "Were you and Heather intimate just before you left Hades with Lila?"

He had never been in the habit of kissing and telling. Not even to the brother he'd once adored and whose respect he desperately wanted to win back. "That's none of your business."

"No," Shayne agreed, "it's not." His next words set the wheels in motion to rock Ben's world. "But it might be Hannah's business."

Looking over his shoulder toward the door of the

room where the little girl lay, Ben decided to take this conversation farther away from possible exposure. He moved down the corridor and lowered his voice. But not his irritation. It had been a very long, emotional day and he felt about as close to the breaking point as he ever had professionally.

"What the hell are you talking about, Shayne?"

"Your blood type is B."

He already knew that, having donated more than his share of blood over the years. "So?"

"Hannah's is AB positive." Shayne watched his eyes for a reaction as he spoke. "Her mother's A positive."

Ben banked down a wave of irritation. "Joe was her—"

Shayne cut in. "Joe's blood was O. I typed him when I was trying to save his life after they dug him out of the cave-in." He enunciated every word carefully. "There's no way he was the father of that little girl. And Heather was as shy as they came." He got to his point. "But she did light up like a Christmas tree every time you were anywhere in the vicinity.

"Did you sleep with her around the time that you left?" Shayne repeated. He saw the color drain out of his brother's face at the same time the confusion came into it. He had his answer. "You did." Another piece fell into place. "And you didn't know?" It wasn't quite a question. Ben looked too stunned by the news to have known that Hannah was his daughter.

Shayne's words echoed in Ben's head as he tried to make sense of what he was being told. Of what had to have happened seven years ago. "You think I would have left Heather like that if I'd known?"

"I think that Lila had you so tied up in knots and so crazy about her that there was no telling what you were capable of back then." His eyes held Ben's. "Question is, what are you going to do now?"

Stunned, reeling, Ben didn't know the answer. But he did know that the right thing would be to ask Heather to marry him.

The funny thing was, until just now, he kind of thought that was the path he was on. Making his way toward asking Heather to marry him. Because he'd found himself falling in love with the woman and her daughters. Found himself wanting the kind of life Heather would give him.

The kind of life his brother had.

Home, family, love. Having space taken up in his bed by someone he wanted to see the moment he opened his eyes in the morning.

But now everything was different. Not because a sense of responsibility had brought along a sense of confinement, of being hemmed in, but because Heather had lied to him. She had lied to him with her silence. He'd had a right to know that Hannah was his. Right from the beginning, he'd had a right to know.

And he didn't believe for one minute that Heather had ever thought the little girl was actually Joe's.

There was absolutely no resemblance. Hannah was delicate, like fine china. Joe had been a large, lumbering man with reddish hair. Hair like Hayley's.

She'd been pregnant when he'd left town. That would explain why she had married the miner so quickly. A lot of things made sense now.

And more didn't.

Ben glanced back at Shayne and realized that his brother was silent, still waiting for an answer to the question he'd thrown out. "I'm going to talk to her."

"Maybe now's not the best time."

Cynicism washed over Ben. "There is no 'best' time to talk about something like this."

"She's been through a lot, Ben."

"And I haven't?"

"Heather almost lost her daughter today. She did lose a husband several years back. She's worked herself to a frazzle, taking care of those girls and her mother. You've just had your ego bruised. I know it's a completely new sensation for someone like you, but now you're part of a fellowship in a very big club." The teasing note left Shayne's voice. "Go easy on her."

Ben laughed shortly. The sound rang of irony, not humor. "This is something new, you giving me advice about women."

"Not women," Shayne corrected. "A *woman*. You're smooth and suave and women have always lined up six deep to be with you, but you've never really had a relationship that had deep roots, Ben. That mattered. So, yes, I'm giving you advice because I'm lucky enough to have that kind of relationship in my life."

Ben had no comeback to that. For a second he merely stood there, absorbing what he'd just heard. Shayne was right. His relationship, or whatever there was between him and Lila, had not prepared him for this. It had been based on mutual gratification, on grabbing everything they could from life and from each other. But in the end nothing had been forged, nothing had been built. And what there was, dissolved like a sugar castle in the rain. After a long moment Ben nodded. And then he went back into the room where Hannah was.

Pausing at the door, he took a breath, then turned the knob and walked in.

She was awake.

Hannah's eyes were open. She had green eyes. Green, like his. Why hadn't he seen that before? Why hadn't he seen that when Hannah smiled, as she was trying to do now, she had a dimple in her left cheek, just like he had? Or that her expression, when she was thinking, reminded him of the photograph of him when he'd been a kid, sitting beside Shayne in their parents' living room?

Hannah was his daughter. There was no doubt in his heart. She was his.

A barrage of questions rose up in his mind, on his tongue. He wanted to hurl them all at Heather like rapid gunfire. He wanted to demand why she hadn't told him. If not then, why not now?

But he couldn't ask any of those questions without upsetting Hannah. And first and foremost, the little girl was his patient. Even if she hadn't won his heart.

Even if she hadn't been his daughter.

After sitting close to the hospital bed, he swept away her hair from her forehead, smiling down at her. It would take a while before the color would return to her cheeks.

"Hi," he greeted Hannah softly. "Welcome back. You gave us quite a scare."

The smile on Hannah's lips quivered. She lacked the strength to sustain it. "Hi," she murmured.

She could have died, he thought. Died before he'd ever known that she was his. He felt angry at almost being cheated. And angrier at himself that he hadn't instinctively known right from the start that Hannah was his daughter.

"What made you think you were a bird?" he asked.

The corners of Hannah's mouth drooped. She held on to her mother's hand. "I'm sorry."

He didn't want her to think he was chastising her. He didn't want her to be afraid of him.

"Not as sorry as we would have been if something had happened to you." He leaned in closer over the railing that kept her from falling out. "We all love you, Hannah. Your mom, your sister, your grandmother. And me," he added with a warm smile.

Small, perfect eyebrows rose high on her forehead. "You, too?"

"Me, too," he assured her, giving her other hand a squeeze. "So, I want your promise. No more flying off rooftops." And then he remembered what he'd been like as a boy. A broader range was needed. "Or off anything else for that matter. Deal?"

"Deal," Hannah promised him. The very effort of saying the word ushered in exhaustion. Her eyes began to drift shut again.

Very slowly Heather disengaged her hand from Hannah's. She gently tugged the blanket into place over her daughter. She was far from calm. Calm would take time. But her relief was beyond measure. When she looked over toward Ben, fresh tears sprang into her eyes. "I don't know how to thank you."

"You could start with the truth." He'd decided not to say anything for the time being. But his hurt and anger over the deception had forced out the words.

Heather stared at him as if he'd just lapsed into a foreign tongue. His words made no sense to her. She had been through an entire gamut of emotions today, and fear had yet to recede from her heart. The powerful emotion had had her in a death grip for the better part of the day. Hannah dying was unthinkable. She didn't know what she would do, how she would recover, if she lost Hannah.

Now she wasn't going to. Thanks to Ben, that danger had mercifully passed. But now there was a new threat, a momentarily nameless threat forming right in front of her.

Looking into his eyes, she felt the old dread return. The fear she had always lived with but had managed to bury somewhere beyond reach. A fear that, despite everything, despite the years, was never all that far out of range. The fear that Hannah's true paternity would come out.

"The truth?" she echoed, stalling for time, praying she was just being overwrought and paranoid and that he was referring to something entirely different.

"Why didn't you tell me Hannah was mine?"

She was right. He'd found out somehow. She squared her shoulders as she raised her head defiantly. The time for silence was over. "You were gone. By the time I knew I·was pregnant, you'd left town with Lila."

And that was his fault. On so many levels. But that didn't negate that she'd continued to keep the fact from him after he'd returned to Hades.

"But I'm back now," he pointed out. "And I've been back for two months now. Two months," he emphasized. "And during the last month, we've been seeing each other pretty much on a daily basis." A bolt of anger came out of nowhere and he struggled to control it. He didn't want to frighten her, he just wanted answers. Answers he could live with. "You slept with me, Heather, and you still didn't tell me?"

"One doesn't have anything to do with the other."

"Doesn't it?" he demanded, his voice rising. Ben paused to get it under control. He didn't want

Hannah to hear them arguing. "I thought honesty was part of the equation."

A defiance he'd never associated with her before rose into her eyes. "I didn't lie to you."

"No," he agreed, his voice mocking her, "you didn't come out and say Hannah was Joe's daughter, but you lied to me when you didn't say it. When you didn't tell me she was mine," he said.

He wasn't going to make her feel guilty about that, he wasn't, she thought fiercely. She had her reasons. Reasons that put Hannah before her own desires. "I didn't want to ruin what there was."

He narrowed his eyes, trying to understand. "Between us?"

She shook her head. "No. What there was—is—between you and Hannah."

"How could telling me that Hannah was my daughter ruin something?"

"Because once you knew that she was, you would have felt guilty, or obligated, or wanted to leave town again because you felt hemmed in." She tried her best to make him understand. "You're like the wind, Ben. You come in, rustle leaves, stir things up and then you disappear. And that's okay, because that's you. But I didn't want Hannah ever to think that you were running out on her, that you didn't want to stay to be her father. It would have been hard enough for her to lose you when she just thinks of you as my friend. She's gotten very attached to you. Both the girls have."

And so have I. Me maybe most of all.

"And you're that sure I would run once I knew?"

She chose her words carefully, not wanting to insult him, but not wanting to lie. Especially not now. "Not a hundred percent, no. But I didn't want you 'doing the right thing,' either."

He could only shake his head, bewildered. "I don't understand."

She smiled for the first time. A small, sad smile that went straight to his core. And made him feel like a heel, even though he didn't know why. "No, I don't suppose you do. Most women want to get married for the right reasons."

"The right reasons," he repeated. "Enlighten me. What are the 'right' reasons?"

"Because someone loves you. Because they can't exist a day without you there, sharing a name, a house, a love with them. You don't like being tied down, Ben. Being a father would tie you down." And he would grow to hate her. And perhaps even hate the girls. She couldn't bear that.

Maybe that had been true once, Ben thought as her words pricked his skin, but that wasn't who he was now. He'd changed, he realized. And she needed to know that. "You had no right to make that assumption."

"When it comes to Hannah, I have every right."

"And what about me?" he asked.

Chapter Fourteen

Heather stared at him, confused by his question. "What *about* you?"

"What about *my* rights?" he asked.

The impact of having a child was still hitting him, penetrating his consciousness by layers. He'd played with her daughters, gone with them on outings, had a makeshift picnic in Heather's living room when the rain had washed away their plans for holding one outdoors. But it wasn't the same thing as knowing that the child was his own. His own flesh and blood.

"What about my right to have been there when she took her first step, said her first word? When she needed someone's hand to help her up because she fell down? I missed all that, Heather." And suddenly he felt incredibly cheated. "All because you didn't see fit to tell me."

She struggled to hold back the tears. Struggled not to fall into his arms and cry her heart out. If he only knew. But she raised her head and somehow managed to keep her voice steady.

"You were the first person I wanted to go to when I found out. I was very naive back then," she admitted with a barely suppressed sigh. As if that would have changed anything she had gone through back then. "But you'd already left, and nobody in town knew where you'd gone. Not even Shayne. Only that you'd run off with Lila, leaving him to deal with the woman who was coming out to marry you."

A bittersweet expression played on her lips. She hadn't been naive back then, she'd been a simple-minded idiot who was in love with him. Heather shrugged, looking away. "I would have had to be third in line. Third never wins."

He didn't argue with her. There was no point. The past couldn't be resurrected to replay events.

"And Joe?" he asked. "How did he fit into all this?"

Her heart twisted a little with guilt, the way it always did when she thought of the man. "Joe was a very sweet man who'd asked me to marry him once before. When he asked again, I jumped at the chance." She looked at Ben. "I did it to make sure that the baby I was carrying under my heart wouldn't be known around town as Ben Kerrigan's bastard."

He had that coming, he thought. Even so, it hurt. His eyes remained on hers. "Did you love him?"

Heather glanced away as the thorns of guilt grew larger. "None of your business."

He took hold of her shoulders, forcing her to turn toward him. To look him in the eye. "Did you love him?"

She shrugged out of his grasp and pulled away, moving to the far end of the corridor. Her voice echoed through the empty clinic. Darkness had finally settled in around the building. "Why would that matter to you? You've loved a whole legion of women."

"No," he said sharply. "I've made love to more than a few women—although not a legion—"

"Obviously math was never your strong point."

He continued as if she hadn't said anything because he wanted to get his point across to her. "But I've only been in love, or thought I was in love, once." He held up a single finger to emphasize the point.

"With Lila."

He dropped his hand to his side as he nodded. "With Lila." It occurred to him, as he told Heather this, that the ache was gone. That ever-present, saber-sharp ache in his gut when he thought about Lila, about losing her, was gone.

And Heather was responsible for pushing it away.

"What about Sydney?" she asked. "She came out here to marry you."

There was a fondness pervading him as he recalled that segment of his life. Six months spent in correspondence because of an article he'd written about Alaska. The article Lila had read and sought him out to comment on. His now-sister-in-law had turned out to be a singularly wonderful woman, every bit as unique as she seemed in her letters.

"What Sydney and I had was on paper, from another era. I think we each filled a void in the other at the time." Sydney had been getting over a bad relationship and he'd been secretly hurting over one of his own. "Mine revolved around Lila and when she came back…" His voice trailed off as he lifted a shoulder in a half shrug. "I'm not defending what I did."

"No?" She forced herself to dwell on his negative attributes, knowing that otherwise she would melt into his arms. And they'd both be lost.

"No," he replied firmly. "I'm explaining. I know it wasn't right, and I've tried to make amends to Sydney—and to Shayne—any way I know how." Of the two, Shayne had been the harder to win over. Sydney had absolved him from the first. But Shayne was only coming around just now.

"Lucky for you that turned out well for both of them." She smiled enviously as she thought of the couple. "I'm not sure I've ever seen two people more genuinely in love than Sydney and your brother."

Her breath froze in her lungs as he stepped closer and took her hands in his. "I think we could give them a run for their money."

For more than a beat she stood there, speechless. Wondering if she was hallucinating or had fallen asleep by Hannah's bed. But she could smell the musky scent of his cologne, feel the heat of his hand as it held both of hers. That meant this was real. Didn't it?

Heather blinked. "I'm sorry, the shock of this morning—I think I've lost my hearing."

He grinned that engaging grin, the one that always sent her pulse soaring. "You didn't lose anything, Heather. You heard me. I think we could give Shayne and Sydney a run for their money."

"How?" The single word squeaked out. Concentrating, she drew air into her lungs before she passed out. She wasn't going to make a fool of herself, certainly not before he delivered the punch line. She was positive there had to be a punch line.

"Because I love you, Heather. And I have a very strong feeling that you still love me, so—"

Breaking the connection, she took a step back, away from him. "So," she said, emphasizing the last word he'd said, "you're delusional, Ben. And I don't really know what you're up to, or if this is some kind of amusing way to pass the time on your part, but—"

He took hold of her wrist to keep her from moving away any farther and broke through her barrage of rhetoric. "Marry me, Heather."

Silence swallowed up the words. Even the sound of their breathing. If he only knew how many times she'd daydreamed this very sequence of words....

With her last ounce of strength, she summoned her flagging courage. "No. You're asking for the wrong reasons."

The refusal rocked him. A moment ago, he'd been so sure he could break through her resolve. Been so sure that no matter what Heather pretended to the contrary, she loved him. "I'm asking because I love you."

She didn't believe that for a minute. "You're asking because you feel guilty or because you think it's the right thing to do or because you want to try playing husband." The tension in her voice grew. This wasn't what she wanted, but it was what she knew was right. "I don't know which it is, but you're not asking me because you—" She shook her head as he reached for her again. "No, I won't believe you."

He was completely dumbfounded and bewildered. "Why? Why is it so hard to believe me?"

She threw up her hands. "Because you're Ben Kerrigan. Because you've said the L word to half the women in Hades. Because it comes too easy for you."

He hadn't told half the women in Hades that he loved them. Not in the way it counted, he amended. But to argue the point with her seemed futile right now. "Love should be easy."

"No," she countered fiercely, "love is hard. Love is pain. Love is doing what needs to be done instead of what you want to do." She thought of her love for her daughters. "Love is sacrifice and being there in the middle of the night when everything is falling apart." She pressed her lips together as she looked at him. Heather slowly shook her head. "You have no idea what love is."

"So teach me. Show me." Though she resisted, he took Heather's hand and placed her fingertips over his heart. "Feel that?"

It was all she could do to keep her knees from buckling. She loved him. She had for a long time and she always would. But that wasn't enough and she knew it. "Yes."

"It's yours, Heather," he told her. "Yours to do with what you will."

"All right." Taking in a deep breath, she took her hand away. "Then I give it back to its owner."

The next second she was turning on her heel and hurrying back into the exam room where Hannah lay sleeping. Reaching the room, she shut the door with unsteady hands.

Leaning her head against the door, she fought to regain some kind of composure. She prayed that Ben wouldn't come into the room after her because she only had so much strength to turn him down.

She had to think of the girls. Even though Ben might mean what he was saying—or think he meant it—for the moment, as certain as the sun was going to rise tomorrow, his attention span would begin to wander.

Or Lila would come waltzing back into town, crook her little finger and take him away again.

She couldn't put the girls through that. Couldn't have the girls love him and then watch as he left them. It would be too awful for them.

Never mind what she would feel.

The sound of a door creaking caused Heather's eyes to pop open and her body to tense moments before she was fully conscious.

Daylight streamed through the back windows, but that hardly meant anything. Daylight arrived at an ungodly early hour in the summer and remained unfashionably late.

Squinting, Heather tried to make out the numbers on her wristwatch. Six-thirty. She'd intended to keep vigil all night, but obviously she'd fallen asleep. Every bone in her body was now protesting the indulgent slip. The chair she sat on was uncomfortable enough when it came to sitting. As far as sleeping went, it was a modern-day equivalent of a torture rack.

Shifting, taking care not to pull a muscle, Heather looked over her shoulder. She'd expected to see Ben and was surprised to find Shayne entering the room.

Crossing to the bed, Shayne nodded at Hannah, who was just beginning to stir. "How was her night?"

"She slept right through. Not a peep out of her." She was certain she would have heard something if Hannah had woken up. Her mother instincts, honed when the girls were first born, were too keen not to.

He smiled at the little girl. Color was returning to the thin cheeks. And her eyes looked a lot brighter. "Well, Hannah looks a lot better for her night's sleep." Picking up the chart to make a few notations, he said offhandedly, "You, however, look like you should go home. I could call Max to take you." He knew the sheriff wouldn't mind.

Heather rose on legs that felt just this side of wobbly. Maybe she should go home to get a little sleep now that everyone was returning to the clinic.

"No. No need to bother anyone. I can drive myself home." And then she hesitated.

Shayne saw the question in her eyes, knew that pride was stopping her from asking it out loud. He was well acquainted with pride. Pride had turned him into a stubborn, almost reclusive person until Sydney unlocked his prisoner door. "He's not here."

Heather squared her shoulders. "I didn't ask."

"No, but I thought you should know."

And then she read between the lines and realized what Shayne was actually telling her. She could feel her heart constricting in her chest.

Your own fault. You sent him away, remember?

"You're not talking about just the clinic, are you?" Each word tasted bitter on her tongue.

"No," he replied quietly. Then with more feeling

he added, "He said he had to go to Seattle for a few days, to see about some things. Asked me to check on Hannah." He looked across the room. The girl was dozing again. "As if I wouldn't without being asked."

The smile on her lips was only a token response to his last sentence. "Everyone knows that you're the very best there is, Shayne." And then, even though she told herself not to, she heard herself asking, "Did he—did he say why he was going?"

Shayne shook his head. Ben had come to him almost in the middle of the night, knocking on the door until he came down the stairs to open it. He'd never seen Ben look that way before, as if he'd been up all night, wrestling with something that was bigger than he was. He'd listened in silence, at first condemning Ben, then realizing that his younger brother was hurting and trying to deal with it the best way he could.

"He told me he didn't want to go into that just now. But that he'd be coming back."

Sure he will. Just before the Second Coming. She blew out a breath. "Do you believe him?"

"Yes." Shayne looked at her. Her feelings were right there, in plain sight. "But you don't."

She slid her tongue along her lips before shaking her head. "No."

And then Shayne did what he'd thought he would never do. He became Ben's advocate. "Ben's changed since he got back, Heather. He's tried very hard to prove himself to me. And to himself, I suspect. To prove that he isn't the same carefree Ben Kerrigan anymore. That he has finally grown up."

She supposed she couldn't expect Shayne to say anything else. After all, Ben was his brother. She shrugged, trying her best to seem unaffected. And probably failing miserably, she thought. "So now he proved it to himself and he's moving on."

Shayne surprised her. He ceased playing along. Instead he turned her face toward him. She could feel his eyes scrutinizing her.

"What happened here last night?" She pressed her lips together harder, to keep the tears from springing to her eyes. "It won't leave this room," he promised. "You can ask Sydney," he added with a soft chuckle. "I drive her crazy because there are things I can't tell her." His eyes held hers. "Things that are just between a doctor and his patient."

"I'm not your patient," she reminded him.

Instead of saying anything, Shayne took a tongue depressor out of his pocket and held it at the ready. "Say 'ah.'"

Confused, she did as she was asked. Tilting her head back, she said, "'Ah.'"

Shayne went through the motions of looking down her throat. Satisfied, he tossed the tongue depressor into a wastepaper basket. "Okay," he informed her, "now you're my patient."

She smiled and shook her head. Shayne meant well, but she just couldn't talk about it. But when she opened her mouth, somehow the words came tumbling out. "Ben asked me to marry him."

That surprised him. But then, the proposal was in keeping with the "new" Ben. And it meant that he'd been right. "Then Hannah *is* his."

Her eyes widened. "You knew?" How long? Had he known right from the start, when Hannah had been born? Who else knew?

She looked shaken, and he wanted to comfort her. But he knew this was something she had to work out for herself.

"Only that Joe was the wrong blood type to have fathered that girl." He kept his voice low, even though they were on the opposite side of the room. Neither one of them wanted Hannah overhearing. This was something that had to be told to her the right way. "And I knew what Ben's blood type was."

"How long have you known?" Her voice quavered.

"Just since yesterday—and not for certain until just now." He paused for a moment, searching her face again. "I take it you didn't say yes when Ben asked." She shook her head. It didn't make any sense to him. He'd seen the way she'd looked at Ben. The woman was clearly in love with him. And Ben with her, if he was any judge of the human condition. "May I ask why?"

She knotted her hands before her and looked down at them. "When Joe asked me to marry him, I knew he loved me. Ben was asking because he felt he had an obligation." She raised her head, tossing it as she looked at Shayne. "Ben doesn't love me. And I'm not about to take advantage of the situation."

"You did when Joe asked you. You didn't love him," he said. She glanced back up at him, clearly taken aback by his assessment. "When a woman is carrying the child of the man she loves," he elaborated, "she acts in a different way than you did. There was a discomfort, a guilt in your eyes. I always thought it was just because you didn't love Joe, that you'd married him to help you take care of your mother. I didn't realize you'd married him because you needed a father for your baby."

"I made it up to Joe," she said defensively. Old memories rose up, bringing with them old guilts. Demons she'd wrestled with time and again. "I was the best wife to him that I knew how to be. He knew I didn't love him the way he loved me, I never tried to hide it." It was there, unspoken but understood, like a white elephant in the living room. "But I did love him," she protested. "I loved him for his kindness, for his generosity of spirit...."

He knew that wasn't enough for any man. And it wasn't fair to either one of them. "You could have come to me," he pointed out gently. "I would have helped you. You didn't have to marry Joe."

"Thank you, but I couldn't have come to you. I don't take charity," she told him proudly. "Besides, I wasn't going to have people whisper behind their hands about Hannah. No," she informed him firmly, "my way was better. My way Joe had a family and Hannah had a father. Everyone was happy."

He looked at her knowingly. "Except you."

The shrug was careless, dismissive. This was the greater good for the greater number. "I love my daughters. That's enough."

He got down to the salient point. "Why are you so sure that Ben doesn't love you?"

That was very simple. She wished it wasn't, because then maybe she would have missed the truth. But there it was in front of her in neon lights.

"Because he didn't ask to marry me before he knew about Hannah. And then, suddenly, a proposal was popping out of his mouth. No." She shook her head, struggling with tears all over again. Damn it, wasn't that ever going to stop? "He was just trying to do 'the right thing.'" She tried to sound philosophical. "Well, so am I. I don't want Ben to marry me out of a sense of obligation. I don't want to look at him in a year and see that he's miserable because he wants to be somewhere else and can't because he's anchored down by a family."

In his estimation, she was missing something very basic. "Did it ever occur to you that Ben might want that anchor? That feeling of staying put?" He thought of what Ben had said to him a few weeks ago, that he envied him his life. What Ben envied, what Ben wanted, was a family of his own. And now Heather had turned away from him.

"No," she replied truthfully. "It didn't. Because that's not Ben."

Shayne started to argue but never got to make his first point.

"Mama?"

The small voice sliced through the conversation, wiping everything else from Heather's mind except for her daughter. Instantly she hurried back to the bed and the small figure lying in it.

Summoning her brightest smile, she looked down at the precious life that had almost been taken from her. "Right here, pumpkin."

"You, young lady," Shayne admonished, following Heather over to the bed, "were almost pumpkin pie yesterday." He gave her a semistern look. "I always thought of you as the sensible one. What happened?"

Hannah's voice grew very small. "I got tired of hearing Hayley say I'm a baby. That I'm scared of everything."

"Being scared of breaking your neck is a very good thing in this case," Shayne told her. "No more flying lessons, deal?" He put out his hand to her.

Hannah slipped her small hand into his, a hesitant smile shyly blooming on her lips.

"Deal," she murmured. And then she looked at her mother. "Can I go home now, Mama?"

"Not yet," Shayne told her. "We'll see about that

this afternoon," he added when she looked too sad for words. "But you have to promise me to stay in bed and do everything your mother tells you to."

Hannah solemnly nodded her head. "I promise." Her eyes scanned the room. Clearly she didn't see what she hoped to see. "Can I see Dr. Ben now?"

Heather felt her heart twist in her chest. "He's not here, honey," she began.

"He had to go to Seattle for a few days," Shayne quickly said.

"But he'll be back?" There was a note of uncertainty in the question and the kind of sadness that only a child who had gotten attached could summon.

This was where she had to start laying the groundwork, Heather thought. In her heart she felt certain that Ben wasn't coming back. That finding out Hannah was his had shocked him enough for him to want to leave after he'd thought the matter over.

"I think that—"

"Sure he'll be back," Shayne assured her, cutting Heather off. "In a few days. Or maybe a week."

Or maybe longer, Heather thought. A lot longer.

Chapter Fifteen

"Why don't you come with us, Heather?"

The irony of the invitation made Heather smile despite what she was feeling. It had come, not from Ursula, who seemed to have made a regular habit of stopping by the house these days, but from her mother. Her reclusive, sour-dispositioned mother. The very same woman who had spent all of her adult life seeing the glass not only half empty but cracked and about to shatter. Bit by bit she had transformed into a person who now looked at each day as one that had definite potential. That teemed with hope.

Moreover, her mother was dating, actually

dating. Or, to put it in the terms her mother preferred, "keeping company."

Whatever she chose to call it, Martha Ryan was seeing a man on a very steady basis. Yuri's cousin Jan had decided that living in Hades suited his purposes just fine, and he had moved into the old Fitzgerald place. Her mother had even gone to see it on several occasions. And stayed the night twice.

It did Heather's heart good to see this. Which was fortunate because the state of her heart was not too good otherwise. It felt pretty beaten up and battered for the past month.

At least there were some miracles left in the world, Heather mused. In that area, she supposed she really shouldn't complain. Hannah had recovered and was back to her old self. That in itself was a miracle. When she allowed herself to think of what might have happened to the little girl, her blood ran cold. As for Hayley, her last born was properly contrite these days for her part in her sister's accident and still very eager to make amends. She couldn't do enough for Hannah.

Both girls had finally ceased asking her when Ben was coming back. They seemed to instinctively sense that whenever she said, "I don't know," her heart hurt to the point that she could hardly stand it.

She was still struggling to make herself accept the obvious.

He wasn't coming back.

She knew that, and still she waited, still she

hoped, although much less than before. One day had gone by, then two, then three, until a lonely week had formed. It dragged another in its wake, knitting together until somehow, inexplicably, a month had gone by. A month and still no Ben.

Why couldn't she just accept that and be done with it?

"Heather," her mother was saying, bringing her wheelchair around so that she was directly in front of her, "I don't want you rattling around in this house by yourself again tonight."

Heather's mouth curved. She couldn't remember her mother ever being this thoughtful, this concerned. Being in love was obviously good for her. "It's hardly big enough to rattle in, Mother. Besides, it's nice to have some time alone."

Martha exchanged glances with Ursula. "Not when all you do is think and brood," Martha chided, the old reproving note back in her voice.

Funny, Heather couldn't help thinking, that could have been her talking to her mother not three months ago. But that had been before Jan had come into her mother's life. And Ben back into hers.

Only difference was, Jan was still here.

Martha looked torn. She glanced at Jan. He nodded, as if he could read her thoughts and gave his approval.

"Maybe with the girls sleeping over at Ike's house, I should stay home," she offered.

Touched, Heather could feel tears forming. She

dug her nails into the palms of her closed hands, willing the tears back.

"No, you should not," she informed her mother firmly. She appealed to the tall, muscular Russian. "Jan, help me out, here. Please take your girlfriend and go," she entreated.

But even Jan looked a little hesitant. "You will be all right?" he asked, his voice kind.

If she gave even the slightest indication that she wasn't going to be "all right," Heather knew she was going to have four people hovering over her. And while she was grateful for the display of concern, all she wanted to do was be left alone to grapple with this monkey on her heart as best she could.

She needed time, that was all.

It wasn't as if she hadn't seen it coming. From the very first moment she saw him at the clinic, she'd been bracing herself for Ben's departure. At least this time she wasn't pregnant. This time all she'd wound up nursing was a broken heart.

"I'll be fine," she assured Jan as his dark eyes seemed to delve into hers. "Really," Heather underscored when she found herself the focus of not one but four sets of eyes. She was not about to stand still for pity, however well-intentioned. "Now go," she ordered, shooing them toward the door. "Beat it. I mean it."

"Bossy little thing," Ursula commented to Martha as Jan got behind the wheelchair and began to push

Martha toward the front door. She smiled as she looked over her shoulder at Heather. "Reminds me a great deal of April."

The door finally closed as Yuri pulled it shut behind him. Heather allowed herself a loud sigh of relief.

It echoed back at her in the empty house, bringing with it a fresh wave of loneliness.

She shoved her hands into the pockets of her jeans, not moving another muscle. The evening stretched out before her like a darkened desert with no discernible shape, no form whatsoever.

Hannah and Hayley were at a sleepover and, with her mother finally out, she had the entire evening all to herself.

To do what?

She had to *do* something, Heather insisted silently, refusing to spend another minute devoted to self-pity. She had a life and she had to get on with it. Spending another moment waiting for a knock on the door was just stupid because—

Heather stiffened.

Someone had just knocked on the door.

Could be anyone, she told herself. After all, she wasn't a hermit. People occasionally did drop in on her. Especially now with Ben gone. Everyone and his brother in Hades seemed to think she needed cheering up. As if she were some lost waif they'd taken in.

Well, she wasn't a waif, she was the mother of

two and a woman who would go places eventually. Since Ben had left so abruptly, she had made herself enroll in an on-line college and was finally taking courses toward that degree in art that she'd always wanted to get. Maybe once she had her degree, now that her mother looked as if she was going to be taken care of, she and the girls would leave Hades, try someplace new. Someplace where she would be too busy to let herself dwell on Ben.

The knock came again. Crossing to the door, Heather twisted the doorknob, opening it.

Her mouth dropped open.

He filled her doorway the same way he had filled her heart. Completely.

It took her a second to find her tongue and get it in gear. "Ben?"

He flashed her a grin, doing his best to hold on to the gift he'd brought. The gift had other ideas. It scrambled up his shirt, licking its way to the top. Tightening his hands around the plump middle, Ben eased it down again. "Hi. The girls around?" He glanced about the area as he asked. "I brought them a puppy."

"Ben," Heather repeated, as if to convince herself that she wasn't looking at a mirage, or a ghost from her not-too-distant past.

"Yes." He inclined his head, amused. "I think we've established that." And then he laughed because the Labrador puppy, in another attempt to scale his chest, was licking him so hard she was tickling him.

It was hard for Heather to process anything when her brain had gone numb. She struggled to sound coherent. "What are you doing here?"

"Trying to give the girls a puppy," he said, laughing. Grasping the dog firmly by the middle, he set it down on the floor. The dog instantly began to explore and sniff, sealing everything into its memory banks.

She didn't know whether to scoop up the puppy and shove it back into his arms or just slam the door in Ben's face. Four weeks. Four whole weeks and not a single word. Who the hell did he think he was, putting her through that?

Her eyes narrowed as she stared at him. "You can't do this. You can't just waltz back after a month and bring someone a puppy and think that everything's going to be all right just like that." She snapped her fingers to underscore her point.

"I know that," Ben replied quietly. His eyes were looking into hers. Looking into her soul. Stepping over the threshold, he pulled the door shut behind him, never taking his eyes off Heather. "I know it's going to take work. And time." Once again he scanned the immediate area. The puppy was sniffing Hayley's doll on the floor. "Are they…?"

"They're at a sleepover," Heather informed him tersely, chagrined at her loss of control. She struggled to reclaim her composure.

Dragging her hand through her hair, Heather felt utterly confused and torn. She wanted to beat on him and throw her arms around his neck at the same time. With effort, she forced herself to focus on the dog. It was the kind of dog that the girls had been after her to get, pleading until they ran out of collective breath. She'd remained firm, saying that she had enough to take care of. But now that the puppy was here, she couldn't continue saying no. Not to a sweet, loving puppy that seemed to be all feet and enthusiasm.

Remember what he's done. Remember how you feel.

Her eyes narrowed and she fisted her hands at her waist. "Do you have any idea how much they've been asking after you? How many times they asked me when you were coming home?"

He had the good grace to flush and look guilty. A little. "I had something to take care of," he told her.

Or someone, she thought, at this point confident that the lure of another woman had drawn him away. But that was no concern of hers, she insisted silently. She had to get him to leave. Her heart couldn't take this emotional volleyball. "Look, I know I have no right to be annoyed. I also know that you are your own person and that there's nothing between us—"

"Nothing?" he demanded incredulously, cutting in. "You call that month we spent together nothing?"

"I call it wonderful," she snapped, "but it obviously didn't mean anything to you—"

"I asked you to marry me," he reminded her.

But actions spoke louder than words, and his had spoken volumes. "You disappeared. For a whole month. You've been gone a whole month," she repeated. She drew away, not wanting to be close to him. Not trusting herself to be close to him. Already crazy thoughts were filling her head. And desire was seeping into her veins. She had to be strong. "Is that how it's going to be? Here one month, gone the next?"

"Why are you so angry?" he asked.

She realized that she was shouting. She consciously brought her voice down. He was confusing her. "I don't know."

"I do," he told her. He framed her face with his hands. "It's because you love me."

With effort she drew her head away. It would have taken a great deal less for her to remain just where she was. To let nature take its course. And then, tomorrow, she would have to wage this war within herself all over again. "Look, Ben—"

"Which is okay," he went on as if she wasn't trying to cut in, "because I love you."

Her eyes narrowed into angry slits. She expected more of him. "Men who love women don't disappear for a month without calling them."

There was a reason for that. And it had been hell maintaining his silence, because all he'd wanted to do was just hear the sound of her voice, to feel the softness of her body.

"I wanted you to miss me." He took a breath, steeling himself off. "Or find out that you didn't. Either way, I thought things would move along better without me here for a while. Besides," he repeated, "I did have something to take care of."

Heather decided to call his bluff. "What?" she asked, fully expecting him to stumble his way through a lie.

He could almost read her thoughts, he realized. That happened when two people were in tune with each other. The thought heartened him. "I belonged to a very upscale practice before I came back to Hades."

"And you wanted to see if they would take you back," she guessed. Even as she tried to maintain an angry facade, she could feel her heart sinking. Feel him figuratively moving farther and farther away from her. It hurt like hell to be right, she thought.

"No," he contradicted patiently, "I went there because I wanted to see if my old partners would help me with a fund-raiser."

She repeated the words, although for the moment it made no sense to her. "A fund-raiser?"

He nodded. "In case you haven't noticed, things are not exactly state-of-the-art at the clinic." There was a whole host of things they needed, but he began with the ones he'd targeted this time. "Among other things, we need an MRI machine. We need an operating room that doesn't do triple duty as a recovery room and an exam room."

Heather stared at the expression on his face. Ben was serious. He was really serious. "So you held a fund-raiser for that?"

"Yeah." He grinned, thinking of the final amount that he had personally tallied. He'd gone on to collect the pledges himself, depositing them into an account he'd opened for the clinic at his old bank in Seattle.

"We did pretty well, too. I stopped by and gave Shayne the check before coming here." It was a tough call to say whether Shayne looked more surprised to see him back, or to see the check Ben had handed him. Shayne had been speechless. Not that his older brother had ever been all that talkative to begin with, Ben thought fondly.

"Seeing as how he's in charge of the clinic," he continued, "I figured that he'd want to be the one to have final say on the machine. And the plans to expand the clinic."

It all sounded so incredibly selfless. And just the way she'd always dreamed he'd be. But dreams like that belonged to an adolescent and it had been a long time since she'd been that.

Heather looked at him for a long moment. "You did all that?"

"Yes."

"Why?"

He shrugged. It should have been self-explanatory, he thought. "Because I've gotten accustomed to the best, and if I'm going to stay here, I want conditions at the clinic to be less primitive. Hades is growing." Humor twisted his lips. "There are at least ten more people here now than there were when I left seven years ago." He struggled to keep a straight face, but he lost.

The grin went right to her heart. She was lost and she knew it, but she tried to maintain the charade a little longer. "So you're staying."

Ben nodded. "That's what I said."

Out of the corner of her eye, she saw that the puppy had made friends with what looked like Hannah's old slipper. The animal must have retrieved it from under the sofa. Right now, the puppy was getting to know her new friend. From the inside out.

Heather gave a quick, careless shrug of her shoulder. "The girls will be happy."

He took a breath. This was going to be slow going. "I'm through with that part of my life, Heather, I—"

"My girls," she emphasized. "Hannah and Hayley. My girls will be happy to hear that you're staying."

"Oh." He flushed ever so slightly beneath his tan. "I thought you meant—" And then he waved his hand at the error, dismissing it. "Never mind what I thought." Before he suddenly got tongue-tied for the first time in his life, Ben decided to take no chances. Reaching into the front pocket of his jeans, he took something out. "I also went back to Seattle to get this."

Holding his hand out to her, he uncurled his fingers. The overhead light caught one of the surfaces of the diamond ring in his palm, throwing out bright prisms that streamed about the room. Heather caught her breath.

He watched her face for a reaction. "I know I'm repeating myself but, marry me, Heather."

It took everything she had, not to grab the ring and put it on her own finger before he changed his mind. Instead she raised her eyes to his. "What if Lila comes back to Hades?"

"She won't."

That didn't answer her question. "But if she does?"

He shook his head. "Won't matter. I told you, I'm accustomed to the best." Leaning forward, he whispered against her ear. "And in case you don't know, that means you."

Say yes, idiot, before he changes his mind. Say yes! But she had more questions to put to rest, and if she didn't do it now, she never would. "You're not marrying me because of Hannah?"

Taking the ring, he slipped it carefully on her finger as he spoke. "Of course I'm marrying you because of Hannah." She tried to pull back, but he went on as if she'd held her hand perfectly still. "I'm also marrying you because of Hayley." Releasing her hand, he looked into her eyes. Seeing himself there. As well as the rest of his life. "And because I love you."

She caught her lower lip between her teeth. Torn. Wanting so hard to believe, yet afraid to surrender. Afraid because if she did, there would be nothing left to rebuild with if someday he did leave her.

"I'm sorry, Ben, I find it hard to believe that you love me."

A wicked grin curved his mouth. "I could show you. I've thought about nothing else these last thirty days but showing you," he confessed, his voice growing serious. "In every way possible." He ran his hands up and down her arms. "For a long, long time."

Her heart had already climbed up into her throat. "Is this your way of wearing me down?"

The wicked look had worked its way up to his eyes. "How am I doing?"

Okay, so she had nothing left with which to put up a fight. She knew it was time to surrender with grace. Heather slipped her arms around his neck. There was no point in denying that she was his. Because she was. Lock, stock and barrel. "I think you already know the answer to that."

With a swift movement Ben picked her up and swept her into his arms. "God, I hope so. But I'm not taking anything for granted."

She looked at him, very impressed. "That's a new side to you."

"I know." Still carrying her in his arms, he began to climb the stairs. "It's all part of the new, improved Ben Kerrigan."

Would he regret this? Regret settling down? "I didn't ask you to change for me."

"I know. That's why I want to." He paused for a moment to look at her, wanting her to know this above all else. "I want to be part of your life, Heather."

"You can't be part of it, Ben." Holding her breath, she searched his face, searching to see if he understood. She wasn't sure if he did. So she told him. "You can't be part of it because you're *all* of it."

Coming to the landing, he set her down. "But then why did you keep saying no?"

"Because I didn't want to be hurt. I didn't want to feel, indefinitely, the way I've been feeling this last month. But I realized that it's too late. Trying to shut you out doesn't work. I'm already bound to you, already belong to you. So I might as well take advantage of the situation and enjoy whatever time I have with you."

Whatever time. "How does forever sound?"

"It sounds wonderful," she confessed, but she didn't want him making any promises that he couldn't ultimately keep. "But—"

Ben put his finger to her lips. "No, no *but.* Forever it is. Forever and always. Because I love you," he told her softly. "Love you to the point that when I think about you, everything inside of me smiles. And when I think of a day without you, there's nothing. No feeling, just a vast emptiness." He framed her face again, thinking how his world began and ended right here, in her eyes. How could he have been so blind all this time? "I don't want that emptiness anymore, Heather. One month was enough. The next time I go to Seattle, you're coming with me."

"Next time?"

He nodded. "I raised a lot of money, Heather, but it wasn't a king's ransom. The clinic's going to need more eventually." He grinned. Life was going to be good from now on. "And I know some very wealthy people with money to burn and in need of a good cause to make them feel as if they were contributing to society. Have the girls ever been out of Hades?"

"No." As far as the girls knew, the only thing beyond the small town was a forest.

He thought of all the things the city had to offer. "Then they're in a for a treat. But right now," he appealed to her, "I'm in desperate need of a treat myself."

She wound her arms around his neck, her heart singing. "Can't have Hades's new philanthropic doctor feeling desperate."

He grinned. "Glad we're on the same page."

She glanced toward her room down the hall. "I'd rather have us on the same bed."

He lifted her up into his arms again and began walking toward her room. "No sooner asked than done," he promised. And then, to prove he meant what he said and to seal the deal, Ben kissed her. For a very long time.

* * * * *

Don't miss Marie Ferrarella's next romance, CAVANAUGH WATCH, available September 2006 from Silhouette Intimate Moments.

"OH, NO!"

The reaction slipped out before Emma Valentine could stop it, for there stood the very man she most wanted to avoid seeing again.

He didn't look any happier to see her.

"Well, come on, get on board," he said gruffly. "I won't bite." One eyebrow rose. "Though I might nibble a little," he added, mostly to amuse himself.

But she wasn't paying any attention to what he was saying. She was staring at him, taking in the royal blue uniform he was wearing, with gold braid and glistening badges decorating the sleeves, epaulets and an upright collar. Ribbons and medals covered the breast of the short, fitted jacket. A gold-encrusted sabre hung at his side. And suddenly it was clear to her who this man really was.

She gulped wordlessly. Reaching out, he took her elbow and pulled her aboard. The doors slid closed. And finally she found her tongue.

"You…you're the prince."

He nodded, barely glancing at her. "Yes. Of course."

She raised a hand and covered her mouth for a moment. "I should have known."

"Of course you should have. I don't know why you didn't." He punched the ground-floor button to get the elevator moving again, then turned to look down at her. "A relatively bright five-year-old child would have tumbled to the truth right away."

Her shock faded as her indignation at his tone asserted itself. He might be the prince, but he was still just as annoying as he had been earlier that day.

"A relatively bright five-year-old child without a bump on the head from a badly thrown water polo ball, maybe," she said defensively. She wasn't feeling woozy any longer and she wasn't about to let him bully her, no matter how royal he was. "I was unconscious half the time."

"And just clueless the other half, I guess," he said, looking bemused.

The arrogance of the man was really galling.

"I suppose you think your 'royalness' is so obvious it sort of shimmers around you for all to see?" she challenged. "Or better yet, oozes from your pores like…like sweat on a hot day?"

"Something like that," he acknowledged calmly. "Most people tumble to it pretty quickly. In fact, it's hard to hide even when I want to avoid dealing with it."

"Poor baby," she said, still resenting his manner. "I guess that works better with injured people who are half asleep." Looking at him, she felt a strange emotion she couldn't identify. It was as though she wanted to prove something to him, but she wasn't sure what. "And anyway, you know you did your best to fool me," she added.

His brows knit together as though he really didn't know what she was talking about. "I didn't do a thing."

"You told me your name was Monty."

"It is." He shrugged. "I have a lot of names. Some of them are too rude to be spoken to my face, I'm sure." He glanced at her sideways, his hand on the hilt of his sabre. "Perhaps you're contemplating one of those right now."

You bet I am.

That was what she would like to say. But it suddenly occurred to her that she was supposed to be working for this man. If she wanted to keep the job of coronation chef, maybe she'd better keep her opinions to herself. So she clamped her mouth shut, took a deep breath and looked away, trying hard to calm down.

The elevator ground to a halt and the doors slid open laboriously. She moved to step forward, hoping to make her escape, but his hand shot out again and caught her elbow.

"Wait a minute. *You're* a woman," he said, as though that thought had just presented itself to him.

"That's a rare ability for insight you have there, Your Highness," she snapped before she could stop herself. And then she winced. She was going to have to do better than that if she was going to keep this relationship on an even keel.

But he was ignoring her dig. Nodding, he stared at her with a speculative gleam in his golden eyes. "I've been looking for a woman, but you'll do."

She blanched, stiffening. "I'll do for what?"

He made a head gesture in a direction she knew was opposite of where she was going and his grip tightened on her elbow.

"Come with me," he said abruptly, making it an order.

She dug in her heels, thinking fast. She didn't much like orders. "Wait! I can't. I have to get to the kitchen."

"Not yet. I need you."

"You what?" Her breathless gasp of surprise was soft, but she knew he'd heard it.

"I need you," he said firmly. "Oh, don't look so shocked. I'm not planning to throw you into the hay and have my way with you. I need you for something a bit more mundane than that."

She felt color rushing into her cheeks and she silently begged it to stop. Here she was, formless and stodgy in her chef's whites. No makeup, no stiletto heels. Hardly the picture of the femmes fatales he was undoubtedly used to. The likelihood that he would have any carnal interest in her was remote at best. To have him think she was hysterically defending her virtue was humiliating.

"Well, what if I don't want to go with you?" she said in hopes of deflecting his attention from her blush.

"Too bad."

"What?"

Amusement sparkled in his eyes. He was certainly enjoying this. And that only made her more determined to resist him.

"I'm the prince, remember? And we're in the castle. My orders take precedence. It's that old pesky divine rights thing."

Her jaw jutted out. Despite her embarrassment, she couldn't let that pass.

"Over my free will? Never!"

Exasperation filled his face.

"Hey, call out the historians. Someone will write a book about you and your courageous principles." His eyes glittered sardonically. "But in the meantime, Emma Valentine, you're coming with me."

If you enjoyed what you just read,
then we've got an offer you can't resist!

Take 2 bestselling love stories FREE!

Plus get a FREE surprise gift!

Clip this page and mail it to Silhouette Reader Service™

IN U.S.A.	IN CANADA
3010 Walden Ave.	P.O. Box 609
P.O. Box 1867	Fort Erie, Ontario
Buffalo, N.Y. 14240-1867	L2A 5X3

YES! Please send me 2 free Silhouette Special Edition® novels and my free surprise gift. After receiving them, if I don't wish to receive anymore, I can return the shipping statement marked cancel. If I don't cancel, I will receive 6 brand-new novels every month, before they're available in stores! In the U.S.A., bill me at the bargain price of $4.24 plus 25¢ shipping and handling per book and applicable sales tax, if any*. In Canada, bill me at the bargain price of $4.99 plus 25¢ shipping and handling per book and applicable taxes**. That's the complete price and a savings of at least 10% off the cover prices—what a great deal! I understand that accepting the 2 free books and gift places me under no obligation ever to buy any books. I can always return a shipment and cancel at any time. Even if I never buy another book from Silhouette, the 2 free books and gift are mine to keep forever.

235 SDN DZ9D
335 SDN DZ9E

Name		(PLEASE PRINT)	
Address		Apt.#	
City		State/Prov.	Zip/Postal Code

Not valid to current Silhouette Special Edition® subscribers.

Want to try two free books from another series?
Call 1-800-873-8635 or visit www.morefreebooks.com.

* Terms and prices subject to change without notice. Sales tax applicable in N.Y.
** Canadian residents will be charged applicable provincial taxes and GST.
 All orders subject to approval. Offer limited to one per household.
 ® are registered trademarks owned and used by the trademark owner and or its licensee.

SPED04R   ©2004 Harlequin Enterprises Limited

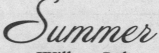

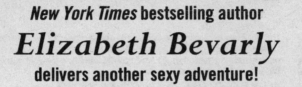

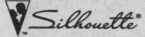
Silhouette®

COMING NEXT MONTH

SSECNM0806

SPECIAL EDITION